Senecus Chronicles

Tales from the Fisher of Time

Douglas P Smith

Kingfisher Press LLC

Senecus Chronicles by Douglas P. Smith

Tales from the Fisher of Time

A book in the Fisher of Time series

Published by Kingfisher Press LLC

Fairview, North Carolina, United States of America

Visit the author's website at www.douglaspaulsmith.com

Cover by MiblArt

This book contains stories of Senecus and his close friends, family, and colleagues. Most are set in the past or present, with a minority set in the future. This book can be read before any of the other books in the series or between books, but some chapters contain spoilers for the book series. Reading this book after *Danu Valley* (book 3) avoids those spoilers.

Portions of this book have appeared in previous books. Those excerpts were rewritten and edited for this version. Those books include: *Resilient* (2021, unpublished) and *Resurgent* (2021, unpublished).

I came from nothing and I'm going back there
But we are all stardust so it will be glorious

Seneca Marcus Aquila (Senecus), 2348

Chapter One

My name is Senecus. At least it is most of the time since I've had to use a few aliases. It is actually Seneca Marcus Aquila, but nobody has called me that the past 1700 years. I'm a completely ordinary guy, with no famous or rich family, no genetics linking me to kings or wizards, or a descendant of any dynasties. In other words, I'm not the Chosen One you run across in a lot of stories, including those that feature light sabers or dragons.

I was just an ordinary soldier doing tedious things in an ordinary place (old Holland) until the vampires showed up. Then the good guys showed up and did something to me, but I didn't know about that until a lot later. Then a goddess showed up to do even more to me, but it was even later that I found that out. I made a friend on Crusade that I had never met, but he had saved me a few times in the past because he was a time traveler. Yeah, I'm still confused about that paradox. All those things happened and conspired to turn me into an immortal that survived the vampire attack which destroyed the Roman Ninth Legion.

I bummed around a lot after my Legion was gone and developed a knack for taking out bad guys. It was profitable because I'd take their money; funny how an awful lot of bad guys had money.

Some I'd keep for myself and the rest I'd give away. It was not much of a life, but I didn't know any better. I was either a vigilante or criminal, depending on the point of view. I suppose I was a practitioner of crime in pursuit of the greater good. Maybe a meaner, sneakier Robin Hood-type. I have done a lot of bad things, but I console myself that I've only acted against bad people. Sometimes serving out deserved fate is an appropriate rationale.

But recently, things took a turn in my life when the top assassin for the Church, Michael, walked into my life. They had found me and thought I'd make an excellent hit man for monsters, and they were mostly right. Along with him came a brilliant research librarian, Jo, that provided quite a few more twists and turns. She really did not like me, so I suppose she was a good judge of character. Or maybe not, since we are now mates.

Quickly after that, I was forced to come to terms with something I'd started but then ignored in America for two hundred years. I had to go back there and face my family of Native American shapeshifters after distant relatives were taken by a river monster. It was not easy thing for me, but that began a cascade of events where I picked up a Bigfoot for an existential tutor, started doing business with Odin, met a seventy-million-year-old original Earthling now ascended to bigger things, and found a twenty-thousand-year-old shapeshifter for a teacher and life mentor.

Then things got interesting. I had a daughter, who was not quite my biological daughter but kind of was, which is a long story, and finally got back with Jo, which was a long story, but then I had to leave them and go to the future to deal with a threat to humanity. My ticket for that ride was getting my head blown off. Good thing I'd learned to shapeshift into a chipmunk.

While up there in the future, I bumped into my oldest friend from our crusading days. He'd been living in the future for quite some time. He was the time traveler that kept coming back into my past to save me before we had ever met. Again, I'm still confused by that loop. But we took care of the threat and eventually we both came back after a slight time hiccup.

Since then, life has been easy being a husband to Jo and father to Isabel, both of whom are smarter than me. Jo can also kick my ass which is good because she is scary enough to keep people from bugging me. I spend my time on some days Doing Things, and other days it's more about Keeping Things Going, which means I get to dabble a lot. Lately I've been working on fae politics to help Morrigan revive that society and helping my daughter Isabel rebuild a spaceship along with my time-traveling best friend Asif. I'm not sure that either Morrigan or Isabel really need me, but they humor me. I'm hoping that Isabel will take me joyriding out to Saturn and Jupiter when she gets the ship finished. Meanwhile we've all relocated to Danu Valley, the safest place in the world. Naming it that made sense after the actual goddess showed up and turned all the waterfalls and creeks into rainbows. Plus, we have the best ice cream flavors. Life is good for this ordinary guy.

But back to work. This book includes my writings and recollections of events in my long life. Plus, I have included stories that others told to me, and through them I've come to learn they have a significant bearing on my life. Or not; some were included just because I liked them. The stories range in time from 65 million years ago to a few years in the future. Although the future stories may not be in your future; depends on when you read this, of course. And on whether time is linear or not. Hint - it is not.

Regardless, the stories are there, the events are mostly true, and even the untrue portions are probably true somewhere in the universe. In other words, these are stories just like any other stories. Enjoy, come over to Danu Valley for a visit, learn to practice a little slant, and we'll be able to turn you into a rodent of your choice in no time.

Chapter Two

Druid

I was given the name Seneca Marcus Aquila at birth, but most centuries I used the variant of Senecus, or just Sen. My given name was properly Roman although my family and I were new citizens of the empire. We were the product of Roman expansion into greater Gaul. Citizenship was granted to good barbarians either sufficiently wealthy or sneaky enough to sell out their barbarian competition.

I don't know exactly where I was born in Gaul, as many towns and villages in northern Europe did not survive to the present day. Even rivers and coastlines have come and gone in that time. Town names also changed, but most were now just rock foundations under three feet of topsoil.

Besides that, imagine going back to a place you visited or lived at twenty years ago. It may not look or feel the same. Now multiply that by a hundred. That is what makes me feel dislocated when I travel around northern Europe anywhere near what I believe to be my point of origin. Of course, there were no accurate maps at the time, and almost none survived to the present. Most maps only included areas important to Rome as they were hand-drawn by Roman surveyors. Later maps were commissioned by the Church at the behest of local authorities or the monarchy. But at the time, most of the best maps were only estimates of the true geography. Looking at an aerial map, I still cannot determine exactly where I was born, nor does it matter. Current boundaries have little to no correlation to the boundaries that existed when I was a child.

Calendars changed a few times over the centuries as well, so the exact year of my birth is also unknown to me. Best guess, as based on my age when I joined the Legion, was approximately 270 AD. But again, as with my birthplace, my exact age is not important. I do know from my mother that I was born in the late spring, likely in the month we now call May.

Ours was a typical family of the time. Grandfather was the patriarch and a schemer, earning his Roman citizenship through shady deals, mostly snitching on his peers. Those snitched upon then faced Roman justice. But Grandfather was intelligent enough to choose those with the least ability to retaliate. He had also provided provisions and scouting reports to the Romans, at least maintaining a façade of a useful person.

My father inherited only the bad side of Grandfather's personality, which was not a good thing for most of the family. Conceited and prickly, he spent his time learning how to scheme, posture, and backstab. But those behaviors only worked for those, like Grandfather, with the wits to know who not to double-cross. My father did not have that gene.

Unfortunately, my two oldest brothers were of the same temperament and became Father's allies. The three of them were unbearable to the rest of us younger siblings after Mother died. The older brother nearest to my age, myself, and my younger sister were taken care of by our older sister. Neither sister was valued much by the patriarch of the family. Stupidly devaluing half of the population is not sustainable, as shown by uncounted failed societies, including mine. But that was Gaul and much of the rest of the civilized world at the time.

Then grandfather died, and my father needed his two oldest

sons for allies. Neither brother had the finesse of Grandfather either, so the trio were doomed to fail. The rest of us realized we were expendable since we were only a drain on father's dwindling resources. My sisters got bundled off quickly to husbands and my other brother died suddenly in a suspicious river accident. I knew I needed to make myself scarce before I was sent to the bottom of the river as well.

My decision to enter the Legion, although underage, was approved of by Father. So much so that he provided the document lying about my age. Probably the only favor my father did for me, and it was a fraudulent letter. But honestly, the Legion was so undermanned they would have taken me without his help. That was how I became a Legionnaire in the Ninth Roman Legion.

After I left the area, my father and brothers lost all their wealth by investing in river trade. Too many of their boats disappeared or were robbed. Likely by the families of those my family had delivered to the Romans. My father ended up working for a landowner for just enough to get by on, with all the money going to food and shelter. One brother died in a boat raid and the other soon found himself hired out to a landowner as well. Despite auspicious beginnings, our family devolved into serfdom in three generations. I rarely saw any of my family afterward. I missed my sisters, but not so much the older brothers.

Why the Legion for me? There were few other choices. Becoming a farmer or merchant required initial investments which were not forthcoming. The priest class did not exist yet in Gaul. I was not afraid of hard work, but serfdom did not appeal to me. Off to the glories of war and conquest for me. I was on my way to what I expected to be a hard life, but fair, with what I hoped was a nice retirement after my service. Once in the Legion, I was tossed in a boat with other new recruits, a couple of veterans, a load of supplies, and we made our way across the channel to Brittania. Being treated like cattle for the crossing was just the beginning of many events that disabused me of any notion of the supposed glories of a soldier's life.

The majority of the men I served with were also simple. Many were like me, from conquered lands and never to see Rome in our lifetimes. Yet the Legion also provided a cosmopolitan environment. We had men from Gaul, Brittania, Hispaniola, in the Legion, but none were from Rome; only some officers were Roman. Also like me, most of the common soldiers would never see Rome. As Rome expanded and the need for soldiers increased, men were recruited from the occupied lands.

Although we were in Brittania, Legion life was the same most everywhere. One commander wrote of my performance after a series of patrols that saw some action. In his opinion I was "brave enough, not stupid." Such faint praise could propel me all the way to middle management in the Legion. But my innermost thoughts were to follow orders, support fellow soldiers, yet always get home safely after the assignment. That made me care little for whatever position I might be given; all were the same unless you were at the top.

People here were like everywhere else, whether in the Legion or in Brittania. Physically, the natives were dark haired with blue eyes, versus people of Gaul, who had green or brown eyes and brown hair. Food was not much different, although perhaps more seafood and local game. I must have eaten an entire warren of rabbits, and to this day won't touch it. But our rations were mostly pork, bread, and sometimes the vegetables that Rome had successfully introduced into the difficult climate.

The Legion officially banned fraternization with the local natives or camp followers. It was likely the least prosecuted rule ever written, unless somebody was stupid and drew attention to that which everyone studiously ignored. Most men knew better as their follow soldiers would suffer if the officers cracked down. But like men everywhere, some got drunk and then fights began between the aggressive and the possessive. Patrols were a way of diffusing aggression in the ranks, although sometimes the locals were easy targets for violent soldiers.

One fine sunny day our patrol went north from Hadrian's Wall near the current village of Brampton. The western end of the Wall tended to be calmer than the Eastern end. It was beautiful summer day, no rain or clouds in site. We would have enjoyed it more if we were not wearing armor and carrying weapons. However, had we not done so and encountered some of the militant locals, we would have enjoyed it a lot less. Getting captured usually meant a few days of torture before your corpse was hung from a tree near one of the Wall forts. The locals did that not to make it easy to retrieve our dead, but because they were proud of their work and wanted the rest of the Legionnaires to see what waited for them beyond the wall. We wanted to return alive and whole, preferably after little to no torture.

The Roman garrison leaders became creative with how they waged retribution. With a nod to both Roman practicality and for the perception that the Druids wielded magic, captured Druids met creative yet gruesome endings. Yet nothing they did changed our behavior, and nothing we did changed theirs. There was no winner in the cruelty competition.

Something not considered by most, and certainly not the entertainment industry, is that the countryside was normally wooded. Deforestation had not come to Brittania yet. A few more centuries, though, and the landscape we see today without trees became commonplace. The Legion did its part by maintaining a healthy clearcut margin of approximately two hundred meters away from the Wall. That kept the enemy archers from sniping the guards and gave some seconds of warning before the blue-painted bastards came screaming out of the trees on a raid. Although they rarely painted themselves blue unless it was a major conflict. Otherwise, it would spoil their camouflage for their normal guerrilla warfare ambushes.

I was one of the youngest and newest, so I got the crap jobs.

Seniority and wealth mattered in the Legion and I was fresh out of both. It made sense though, because the veterans did not want to risk any debilitating injury giving the Legion cause to summarily dismiss them with no retirement. My low place in my own family prepared me for the low life of a new soldier.

We took a road and paths on a routine patrol in an area that had been quiet for two years. No raids, no squabbles, no random arrow shooting in our direction. We visited a small village, a few farms, then moved on to get fresh water. The forest was denser along the small river. Trees at that time could be quite large, with oaks meters in diameter. Our patrol took a break after leaving the river so I was the designated lookout. That was normal per my low status, plus the manner of the lookout post. I got to climb on of the oaks to get a better view of any restless natives creeping up for an ambush. I left my shield and spear below and scurried up to a comfortable branch. The view was not great, but better back then because the forests were more open due to the larger trees and less underbrush.

A half hour into the hour break, I started seeing movement approaching. I estimated at least thirty, greatly outnumbering our ten. I dropped the signal to my patrol below. As the lookout, I carried weighted balls covered with skins of various colors. Dropping those alerted the soldiers below rather than me yelling at them and giving away our location. Especially important because I had no chance to climb down before the guests arrived. My signals told my group the approximate size of the force, direction of approach, and their imminent arrival. Because of training, my guys were on their feet, packed up sans the heavy water skins, and jogging away in less than a minute. My centurion signaled up to me the usual hand signs. They would be waiting for me at a safe place in a clearing nearer the garrison, they'd be back in two hours with more men, and stay quiet until then. Everything I already knew, but officers needed to give orders.

I watched the men leave, and the natives arrive about four

minutes later. They moved like wraiths, quickly and quietly across the forest floor. Against a Roman patrol in the open they would not have stood a chance, but the woods were theirs. Like other raiding parties about a third were female, and all were carrying bows and spears, even a few Roman weapons. They stopped, looked around where we had rested, then moved on to continue the chase.

I tried my best to meld with the tree, hoping none of them looked up. Romans were not known for climbing, so I felt safe enough. But then I saw him walking toward the area as the others left, and instinctively knew I was in trouble. He looked nothing like the descriptions I had heard from my fellow soldiers, but I knew he was a druid. He was not wearing robes, tall, and clean-shaven as I been told they appear. He was normal height, wiry, shirtless, and carrying a strange staff. His long hair was tied back, and his long beard had various small attachments, mostly bones and shells and a Roman coin.

A few feet from my tree he stopped and looked up directly at me. Well, my life had been short and now it was over. The druids were creative torturers and almost always killed Roman captives. I had to decide whether to cower in the tree or drop down to fight. If the others came back, I had no chance, they would fill me with arrows and wait for my fall. At least if I was on the ground, I had a slight chance of running and fighting my way through. I climbed down and dropped the last few feet. I was facing a wood druid, or more likely some sort of warrior priest, so I drew my gladius.

From up close he was not any better looking. But his staff drew my attention. It was a bone, the kind of which I never saw before or since. Nearly two meters long, it had a metal cap on the base, and the top was the knob of bone like that on a femur. Yet the bone was thin and tapered. In my later multiple university stints, I always looked for a bone like that but never found one remotely similar. Probably because it was not from an animal on this planet, at least not in this epoch. But it was a bone with tiny carvings and not petrified.

When I looked at the man, I saw lots of scars a few of which appeared to be earned from combat. Lines of scars were in patterns, possibly symbols, and some contained blue or orange colors. I knew those were ritualistic but had no idea what they meant.

He did not move at all. Just looked at me. I expected him to attack with the staff or call for his companions. But he continued watching me silently with no fear or aggression, but also no compassion. I felt like I was being weighed somehow. We faced each other for a moment, then I felt my skin crawling. Then it stopped and it seemed I woke up. Neither of us had moved but I sensed that some time had passed. He reached up to one of few small leather pouches around his neck and pulled out an object roughly the size of a walnut. Surprisingly he tossed it to me. I caught it and looked at it while keeping him in my vision in case it was a trick. The thing was some kind of bone carved into something I thought might be vaguely amphibious, with a number of tentacles. I had a strong suspicion it was carved from the same bone as the staff.

He raised his left hand and pointed to the side, then pointed to the south, the direction of the garrison. His meaning was clear; I needed to go that direction first and cut south to miss his warriors. It could be a trap, but I had few options. I nodded to him and then jogged off as I put the carving in my belt pouch.

A few hours later, exhausted, I arrived at the garrison. My patrol was already back after not finding me and was rounding up reinforcements. When asked, I told them I had climbed down after the warriors passed but could not get around them for some time, so I was late. I never mentioned the druid or anything of the strange encounter.

The next few nights I had strange dreams. It usually involved water and monsters but nothing specific. I kept the carving until I lost it and everything else after I fell into the river and changed on that fateful night when the Legion died and my life changed.

I never really thought about that carving until recently. Danu and I had spent an evening talking and she had given me a history lesson of her people and herself after the asteroid. Being amorphous, she had the gift of changing form as she described her people we knew as the Makers, after their transition from water to land. The ascended, smoke-like forms I already knew. Then she showed me the physical form she had made to return to the water and wait for millions of years to help humans survive. It was the same as that little carving.

Chapter Three

Charlemagne

I have recounted elsewhere much of my life after I turned into something more than human. Weak, sick, naked, not knowing where I was, barely knowing who I was – those were the terrible early days I remember of my new existence. Then long periods of mundane life, frequent blackouts that lasted for years, with occasional bouts of vigilantism. I lived a few dozen ordinary lives, learned trades, then moved on before anyone caught on that I did not age. This made for an unhappy existence much of the time, as I didn't have a family, nor trusted friends for long.

Looking back, I believe some of those memories are gone or repressed. Chunks of time are missing, whether from the blackouts where I was secretly treated, or just the long span of mundane years with little that was memorable. The 500-year span beginning with my turning at around 300 AD is not always clear in my mind. But I remember enough, or perhaps too much.

I have been asked if I knew famous historical figures or participated in events that are taught in history classes. Mostly no, I did not. One fellow I did see but did not really know was named Charles. He was from a place not too far from where I was born. At first he was a small fish in a big sea of nobles across Europe, full of hundreds if not thousands of appointed, inherited, or self-made aristocrats. But Charles kept trying and moving up the ranks. Later, after I had seen him, he finally got to the point where history gave him the new name of Charlemagne, first Holy Roman Emperor.

How did he move up? He won skirmishes against his enemies, then major battles. Kept his enemies at bay and his allies close. Loyal allies were rewarded, while those that continued to rebel got killed. I don't know for sure, but I suspect he studied and emulated the more successful strategies of the Roman armies and general Roman rule.

Charles was smart enough to not try to expand and rule over new lands with a central army. He kept his forces in various forts around his new empire. They could easily and quickly deal with local uprisings, but several could congregate together quickly into a larger force against enemy armies. To keep his troops loyal, he ensured they were fed, paid, and armed as Charles had the money and wisdom to do so. Camp hygiene was enforced to minimize disease outbreaks. In short, the troops were happy enough to continue being his troops rather than striking out on their own or joining with enemy invasions.

Charles ruled his new holdings according to the behavior of the conquered. He had two major requirements that must be fulfilled; that they convert to Christianity and that they pay taxes. It was not a unique strategy as conquerors had found that imposing very few requirements on the conquered usually was effective in preventing uprisings. Charles used his Christian demand to expand that realm, which curried favor with the pope. The pope reciprocated by eventually naming Charles as the first Holy Roman Emperor. The other demand helped fund his empire expansion, and paid for housing more soldiers on border forts.

Those that paid taxes and kept quiet got protection from enemies on their borders, and occasionally Charles' help when he sent his troops to help the new territory attack the neighbor. They kept oversight over the new land, Charles claimed it as part of the empire, and they split the booty and slaves from the subjugated land. It was popular and profitable to franchise conquest to his newly conquered nobles.

Charles had other means of maintaining his empire. He used his wealth to keep ambassadors at all the conquered territories and paid them well enough to remain loyal. He also sent ambassadors where he could to his enemies, or if not kept spies there. He was kept informed if allies were contemplating rebellion. If they tried it they got put down an his rule reinstated. If they tried it three times, like the Saxons did, thousands were executed. That seemed to bring them around, at lest until Charles died. Those ambassadors and spies also informed Charles of what was happening with his enemies. The knowledge was used to plan and execute military operations. Any bordering enemy having stability problems or disease outbreaks could count on an invading army courtesy of Charles. He was definitely Romanesque in his dealings.

How long did the new empire last? Not long. He made the same mistake from history that other made, including Alexander the Great. He divided up his empire into three parts. I assume he figured that the three rulers would battle it out and the strongest would survive and take over the other two. Sort of what Charles did, when his brother mysteriously died three years after they were appointed co-rulers. Yet if he really did study history, he should have known it wasn't going to work. But perhaps his narcissistic side did not want a successful heir. The next few hundred years the empire expanded and contracted, devolved and evolved, passed through various families, until the Habsburgs grabbed it. It finally and officially was killed by Napoleon.

So how did I know Charles? During those days I still traveled around Holland and picked up different jobs and trades, moving on before everyone around me aged and their children saw me as unnatural. Manual labor mostly, then masonry and carpentry. Charles built a number of estates, palaces, or hunting lodges around his empire, especially in the areas he knew best. One of those was commissioned near the city of Nijmegen, and later the site was known as Valkhof. It was an easy journey south of Utrecht so I decided to get hired as a builder for a couple of years.

Because I had various skills and was not afraid of manual labor the royal contractor was happy to employ me. It was a nice site on a rise above the Waal River. I dug drainage ditches. I assisted with the initial layout of the main house and outbuildings as I could take direction and hold a rope and measure. Along with a large crew we dug the foundations, then began the masonry work to set the base of the walls. Soon we would construct wood scaffolds on the exterior to raise the walls and install wood support beams inside the building. My skills working with felling trees and working as a carpenter kept me in good graces with the contractor throughout the build.

The work camp was well appointed for the times, but sometimes I needed to get away from the other men and spend time in the woods. I would walk until I thought I was far enough away, then begin running at an inhuman pace for a bit. I'd end up at a river or stream and jump in to cool off, then walk back. There were small farms usually closer to the rivers on any high ground that could grow crops above the water table.

On one of my jaunts I encountered a problem. A small group of men had stopped at a small farm that looked new and decided on a game of sport. A young man, really a boy, was roped by the neck next to the wall of a barn structure, with hands tied behind him. Still on horseback, three of them were shooting arrows at the boy. The game was to get as close as possible, even passing through clothing, without drawing blood. The boy already had several grazes as the men had been drinking while riding. It was only a matter of time before they tired of the game or missed and killed the lad. A young girl, likely his mate or sister, was tied up and lying on the ground. She would be next.

Oh well, the Holy Roman Emperor would have to do without four of his finest. I sped at the one off his horse and knocked him down as I drew his sword. The horses were spooked enough that the other three could not get an accurate shot from their bows. A few seconds later they all were headless and dropping from their mounts. The first one I had knocked down was back up with a dagger drawn. I was laughing as I took that hand, then his head. I put another notch in my vigilante belt.

The boy was traumatized, and I doubted he clearly saw what happened or could identify me. The girl was still tied and facing away so I knew she saw nothing. I picked her up and cut the rope around the boy's neck, stashed them both in the barn and cut their hands free. I left them after telling them not to come out for an hour, or ever mentioning the events to anyone. They understood enough to know they would be killed if incriminated in any way with the missing nobles.

Outside I pulled a bag from one of the horses and collected four heads and a hand. Today that sounds like a bad brand of wine. I threw the men across the horses and tied them on. Would not want to litter the woods with bad dead men. Dumping the men and their possessions would not be a problem, but it needed to be far away from this site so the kids would not be suspects. I doubled up two corpses on one horse and I mounted it to get at least a league or two away quickly. The horses I tied together and off we went on our jaunt. Bodies and possessions went into the nearest large river. I kept nothing that might tie me to the men. All the horse livery followed. Now the horses were the problem. I refused to kill and dump them. I rode upriver another league, crossed the river and set them free. Now I had a swim and a long walk back to camp, possibly an all night trip. But the weather was nice, so I didn't mind.

The next month I saw Charles. There had been a minor hubbub over the missing men, but although several people were questioned nobody knew anything. Two weeks after, one horse was found by a farmer and turned over to the authorities. Based on where it was found, the search was conducted far away from where the men were executed or dumped. I had scored another successful vigilante incident. Not for the first time, or last, I wished people would behave better.

Charles was not concerned about the missing men, but rather the progress of his Nijmegen palace. It was going well and he had nothing to worry about. I saw him first on a huge horse, one larger than any others in the group. I guess that was the precursor for a massive SUV. When he got off the horse he looked like any other noble of the time, but he was taller than most. I did not confess to killing four of his lesser nobles, but I did smile at him from a distance. He went on to his fate as a famous emperor and I went on to mine, an anonymous immortal.

Chapter Four

Viking I

After leaving Valkhof I had another blackout. Afterward I moved north, and eventually ended up in Laren in old Holland and tried the family life. That failed miserably and she died after several miscarriages, and I moved on to the coast. That is when I accidentally became a Viking.

I took up residence in a small village called Zuidbert. It was on an island on the eastern edge of the Zuider Zee, the protrusion of the North Sea deep into old Holland. The village is long gone and now polder land, fields of green reclaimed from the sea. I had decided that because of my required nomadic lifestyle, I might as well try out different trades in different places until I either moved on because the locals noticed I wasn't aging, or the onset of another coma took me out of the community. I had continued my fondness for boats and the water and spent more time learning about sailing. What actually happened was the reality of life, and I ended up on a small fishing boat, part of a three-man crew. I had not saved nearly enough funds to live a life of leisure and buy a boat purely for pleasure. Because I liked to eat, although fish wasn't my favorite protein, and could learn to sail somewhat on someone else's boat, I became a fisherman. And then an amateur Viking.

We were not a specialist boat, so anything in the water that was available and had a ready market back on land was fair game. The two others that owned the boat were cousins and descended from fishermen as well. They knew what to do to catch fish or muck oysters, and when to flee when the storms came across the water. They were excellent sailors, but they did it as part of their profession rather than pleasure. But over time, I learned the basics of sailing, made a little money, and never went hungry.

Probably the most amusing thing about the cousins was their names: Peter and Paul. I probably should have called myself Jesus, or at least John, during that time, but felt I did not need to call attention to myself. But most every day there I was, on a fishing boat with Peter and Paul, casting nets, throwing lines, or wading in mud. They were a little older than I looked. Peter was more stocky and Paul was taller, more of what I think of as the modern Dutch look. They were hard workers, sometimes drank to excess, and enjoyed their time off the boat. It was a good job for three years. I had resigned myself to at least a decade there unless the coma came. It ended rather differently than I had imagined.

We had been out most of the morning on a sunny, hazy day further out than normal, fishing on a shoal well past Urk. We were doing well and were already half past full of fish. If luck continued, we would be back well before dark. There was another ship moving our direction in the haze. We assumed at first they were also heading to fish the same shoal. As they closed, however, the shape and size of the boat was wrong. I pointed it out to Peter as he was the eldest of the two, and after a long look, he pulled up all the nets and lines. We quickly made ready and were soon underway, back to the east. The breeze was weak and was not doing us any favors. The other ship had slack sail as well, but then they dropped oars and started gaining on our little boat. Peter and Paul were worried, but I secretly was glad for the chance of a little spat if they caught us.

Another ninety minutes and they were close enough to see

their faces. Further back, we could already tell from the boat they were Vikings. It was early for them, and their ship looked worn with a mended sail and splinted mast. I decided the storms earlier in the week had caught them, and they were looking for an easy score. Otherwise, three fishermen would not have been worth their time. I also counted oars and noted they were about two-thirds of strength. That still gave them twenty men to our three. This might be fun.

Soon they were in bow range and a few arrows thunked into our boat. We did not have any proper weapons other than knives and staves. I would have to change that. Peter wanted to keep running, but we were still a mile to the nearest village port. I was not worried about myself as I could fight my way through this, or worst case, drop overboard, stay down a few minutes, then come back up and swim a mile to shore. My advice to Peter was to give up before we got hit with more arrows, or piss them off since we were about to be boarded. I advised them to pull the sail and let the raiders take the fish since they were likely hungry. So far, they had no reason to kill us. But I worried they were taking slaves and we might look like suitable targets to take back and sell.

Peter relented and dropped the sail. We slowed as they over-took us five minutes later. They looked like a fierce but ragged lot. About an equal mix of the typical made-for-TV Viking look of blonde hair and light eyes, and the actual, more prevalent, dark hair and dark eyes. They threw over two ropes, and we tied them to our boat. A couple were yelling, I surmised, to frighten us or call us awful names; I wasn't sure. The rest were quiet and looked tired and hungry. Five of them, all well armed, jumped down to our boat. Three threatened each of us with sword or hatchet, while the other two checked the boat. There really wasn't anything other than some nice fish. The two then had a quick conference and yelled back over to their ship. The supposed captain yelled back and forth with them for a moment, then the two came up to us and were about to tie us up. I could not let that happen. I guess since there was not much of value onboard, they could at least get three slaves out of their efforts. As one of them tried to grab my hand, I uppercut his chin, spun and elbowed the other in the neck, and continued moving away from the original one that was holding the sword at my front. He stepped toward me as I wanted him to, and I stepped into him, glancing my forearm along the sword to deflect the point, grabbed his right sword hand with my left hand and cold cocked him in the face with my right hand. I now held the sword as he fell and I pivoted to slam the pommel into the head of the one guarding Peter, spinning to backhand the other guarding Paul. All five were down in as many seconds.

As I hoped, the archers had stood down upon our capture and still were not ready to fire. But I was below their boat and was not in a dominant position, either offensively or defensively. That needed to change. The men on the other boat now all had their weapons ready and at any moment, they would throw an axe at my head. I took three long steps and left our deck and landed at the prow of their boat, kicking the one standing there in the head and disabling him. Six down, so at least fourteen to go. Because I was in the narrow prow, only two could come at me at once. The first two rushed forward. I tossed the sword into my right hand and parried the first sword blow, ducked the axe from the other, then kneed the first in the testicles while head-butting the other. Two more down, plus they were also hindering those trying to get at me. Rinse, repeat, two more down. The captain said some more manly Viking words and there was not an immediate rush. Two archers in the back readied instead and then one fired, with the other shooting a second later. I parried the first arrow with the sword and caught the second one, and slammed it into the boat rail. It might come in handy shortly as a thrusting weapon.

About then the captain probably realized his chances of taking me down before I injured his entire crew were slight, plus his authority was in jeopardy. The remaining men were still angry, but self-preservation also seemed to win through the anger. And I imagine the storm had taken a lot out of them. I thrust the sword tip down into the deck to my side and let go of it to cross my arms. I did not know the language but was trying to let them know I could go on all day, but did not really want to continue. The captain stepped forward. He needed to reclaim his place, but without losing face or more men. He was brave or extremely calculating. Exactly what I needed.

We ended up making hand gestures. To make a long and unnecessary story more palatably short, I agreed to go with them as crew, and Peter and Paul were free to go, albeit without most of the day's catch. Seemed like a good deal to me. And that is how I went Viking for a while.

We sailed back north toward the mouth of the Zuider Zee. The crew had been fed, but still the boat was under-manned and not ready to raid any villages in the area. During the first day, through a series of hand gestures with unintelligible words high-lighting the efforts, I learned they were one of nine boats from their region. The storm had scattered them and they didn't know whether the other boats had survived or sunk. Nine boats could easily have raided a series of small villages, so at least for now this part of world was safe.

I kept awake the first night just in case the captain had planned a surprise knife party to end his extra crew member, or if some men were still mad about the earlier beat down. Sure enough, in the middle of the night, three of them tried to rush me with a hide blanket, staves, and knives. In a few seconds, all three were sleeping again the hard way. The captain roused from sleep, glanced over, and said something derogatory. By this time, I hoped the men recognized they were no match and would leave me alone. I had appropriated an old short sword, as it appeared there were extras because of the loss of crew members in the storm. But I did not have to use it on those three.

The next day was nice and breezy and at the mouth of the

Zuider we went east with the wind. There was lots of discussion and gesticulating as the captain and crew were deciding what they could do with one boat. As the day wore on, the weather got worse and decided for us. We headed for a small bay that was protected from the worst of the wind and waves. It was time to be practical and not chance another open water storm. There were a few farmsteads in the bay but no villages, and therefore no plunder potential. We pulled the boat on a shallow beach between rocks and set a sail over the boat to sleep somewhat out of the rain that was soon to come. I walked around a bit to see what the farms looked like. Two of the friendlier men went with me, whether as fellow curious travelers or guards, I was not sure. One man was carrying a bow and as we came to a small stream with a thicket on both sides, a small deer was drinking. He sent a well-placed arrow and the two of them carried the deer back to camp. I was certain they would welcome a roast from that rather than fish again. I kept walking and eventually came to a farm site, with a main house with two outbuildings. A stone and wood fence around one outbuilding had three animals, which, from a distance, could have been goats. I sat by a tree surrounded by bushes and watched the farmstead as the rain began. It seemed there was an older couple, along with three younger people. I could not tell whether they were older children or maybe a younger couple and a sibling. They were getting ready for the evening and closing up everything before the storm.

I needed to warn them of our presence since it was likely my colleagues would plan a morning visit and help themselves to whatever the farmstead could offer. I walked toward the house, then about fifty feet from the front, I stopped and called out. I was far enough that I could spot and dodge an arrow, although the light was failing quickly as the rain came down harder. There was no answer at first, then the door opened and two men came out armed. I saw a third framed in the partially open door with a bow. That was smart of them, and I guessed Vikings had raided them before. I strolled toward the two men with my hands in sight and held off to my sides. That should be clear enough that I was less of a threat. They called out in a language I didn't know, but it sounded similar to Peter and Paul's Frisian. I stumbled through an explanation, with lots of hand gestures, that I was on a Viking boat laid up on the beach nearby, and that there could be a raid later. They seemed concerned enough, but I assume they thought I was insane for coming to warn them.

The younger of the men set out toward the beach to confirm my story, and I stayed outside while the older man went inside. He came back out with a cup of mead and a slice of bread, which he handed to me. I thanked him and consumed both. He asked me something, then I realized he was saying something about me not being a Viking. I agreed and talked and signed that I was a captured fisherman. That seemed to relieve him. A few minutes later, the younger man came back and confirmed there was a boat on the beach. I said my goodbyes as they went into overdrive, gathering up their things and animals to go into hiding. A third man, really a boy, came out and then ran to warn the other farms. I walked back to the beach feeling satisfied that these people would not lose what little they had, and not be pressed into slavery. I was glad for the rain, as it would wash out my footprints in case any of my fellow raiders were paying attention the next morning.

We spent a relatively miserable night with wind and rain coming in around and under the sail covering the boat. The crew was not in too bad a mood as they had eaten the fresh venison. I had no more assault attempts in the night, as I suppose everyone knew it would not end well, or they were saving their violence for the next day. The morning came grey and windy, but the rain had stopped. I was already tiring of the Viking life. The cold and wet was always a part of being a fisherman, but we spent most nights on land in a dry cabin or house. Constant sailing and camping, whether on the boat or on land in a leaky tent, meant there was almost never a dry moment for a Viking. As the men roused, they seemed excited to start the day. After a brief breakfast, we divided into two groups of ten, each heading for the two nearest farms, which were in opposite directions. I was in the group heading for the farm I had previously visited. We hurried off to gather fame and fortune. It was, of course, anticlimactic. There were no people to rape or any goods to pillage or animals to steal. The men seemed depressed. We headed back to the boat to see how the other group had fared.

Back at the boat, the other group was just coming back empty-handed as well. More conversation started amongst the captain and crew. Courses of action as decided by committee; always an awful place to start. We put the sail back up, shoved off the beach, and began sailing to the next grand adventure. Apparently, it was not an uncommon event that once the boat landed, the raid had to begin immediately, or the local people packed up and faded away. Raid me once, shame on you; raid me twice, shame on me. The locals had adapted, and the Vikings needed to find new hunting grounds.

Which was not much of an adventure. Sailing around, dodging storms, staying wet all the time, looking for an opportunity to raid something not too big but not too small, was getting boring. But I was getting to see some of the coastline along lands eventually called Germany, Denmark, and Sweden. But for now, the men grumbled, and all we raided for was food. An occasional farmstead, along with some fishing and hunting. I got to know the men on the boat better and learned just enough language to get along with hand gestures. Most of them were not the firstborn sons in the family, so had not gotten nor would get any farm or land inheritance. Farms and land were the goals of these guys, so they needed to make enough from these ventures to buy their own place. From what I could understand, they said perhaps one boat in ten was lucky enough to make a major haul in a season to allow the crew to go back and purchase property. I would bet it was more like one boat in a hundred. Most of them were living mundane and poor lives, selling out their services at home; going raiding during the season which entailed long bouts of boredom with very occasional exciting and lethal engagements, and hoping someday to buy a place and retire. In some ways, it sounded like a maritime version of the Legion life. But that was all they had, and most of them would die poor and fairly young. I was glad I had killed none of them yet. But I also had no plans on doing a lot of killing for them if we ever found a worthy target.

The men did not seem too curious about me. Mainly, they wanted to know where I had learned to fight. The conversation I found myself in surprised me.

"I learned combat far to the south," I told them.

"On the great warm sea?" one asked. "From the Moors?"

"No," I answered. "On this side of the sea, further inland." It shocked me to learn this poor band of want-to-be farmers knew of the Mediterranean and the people living there.

Some men wanted to spar with me to pass the time. The sword I appropriated was similar in size to a gladius but was more roughly made. Several of the men carried battle axes which were similar but smaller than those I had seen in Gaul. The Vikings were quite good with the axes and I took one up and found that using it in my left hand, with the sword in my right, was quite effective for both offense and defense. Once I learned how to balance and wield it, I felt no need for a shield. After a couple of days, the men started losing interest in sparring, so I stopped beating them and started asking questions about fighting styles of their people and those they encountered. They felt they could stand on their own with any ground troops they faced. They had more trouble with the English with their long range bows, the French with massed crossbows, and in Eastern Europe where large cavalry units operated.

Chapter Five

Viking II

We continued sailing, going north and east along the uneven coastline. The men seemed concerned there were not any other Viking boats on the water. About every third day, we had to beach the boat due to extremely violent storms. Even the one man who had been sailing for twenty years told us this was the worst season he had seen. It seemed an ill omen. But our luck was about to change.

Two days later, we sighted a boat ahead. A larger merchant vessel with no sails left to speak of. We immediately headed toward it like a shark after a wounded fish. As we got closer, there was no movement on the deck. It was not until we boarded that there was a shout, which quickly ended as one of our guys hit the yeller in the head. They found three more men on board and all were already in rough shape from the weather. I could understand that storms had caught them with the loss of several crew and all the sails. Below the smallish deck was a hold filled with trade goods that would never see their intended destination. Cloth, even including silk, barrels of spices, urns of oil, resins and scents. Some boxes of unfinished metal sword and spear blanks, plus copper and tin. And one box of silver. Plus four new slaves. The men were extremely happy.

A discussion began on whether to keep the merchant boat. It would be difficult to sail both since our boat was already under-manned, and the extra sail on board would have to be changed to fit it. And that left us one severe storm away from being stranded with only oar power. Eventually, the captain kept the boat and sent eight men over with the spare sail. We would stay together on the way back to Sweden, but at the first warning of a storm, we would abandon the boat, and bring the sail back. We split the spoils from the hold among the two boats to ensure not all would be lost if one foundered. The more expensive loot and the heavier items we transferred to the Viking boat.

A miracle occurred in that there were no storms for a week and we arrived unscathed, back at the crew's Swedish village , with both boats. The captain split the loot, and they offered even me a share, but I took less than offered. They also asked if I wanted to share a slave, but I declined and told them my people did not keep slaves as a tradition. They were happy to keep the profits for themselves, but I was sure they thought I was crazy.

The village was happy to see the men return with wealth, but there was a solemn moment when the townspeople realized eight of their men were not coming back. But then the party started and everyone headed for the earl's house to drink and lie about exploits. Some people looked at me curiously; I was different, but too well armed to be a slave. I just followed the other men into town and nobody bothered me. They quickly put together a feast and in an hour we were inside a large house and eating and drink-ing. Each man brought his loot in and offered a tithe to the earl. He seemed happy, but kept frowning each time he looked over at me.

The teller of exploits, a man on the boat that was gifted in language, went backward through the journey, with a little embellishment of the huge fight on the merchant boat and the farms raided. Of course, I knew exactly one man got knocked on the head, but they killed several animals one day. He then got to the part where they found me on a fishing boat and I bested almost all the crew but the captain; at least he was fifty percent accurate on that claim. The earl looked incredulous and asked the captain what I assumed was confirmation. The captain nodded and said something back to the earl. He looked unhappier, and I figured trouble was coming soon. I heard the captain say something like 'he looks like a fisherman but fights like a beserker.' Then something about 'not interested in slaves and no trouble unless others start it; good ship mate.' The earl relaxed, but threw a shrewd look in my direction. So, no trouble for now, but I was sure he had something in mind.

I spent a few days wandering around the town. I saw all of it the first day, but I kept moving around to keep from being an easy target. Food was easy to buy and as several of the men had offered me a place to stay, I changed places each night for three nights. Then the captain found me and asked me to come to the earl's hall. He must have finally come up with a plan for me.

I had been thinking about what to do next. Since I had plenty of time, I could spend some years in this area, head to the far east with a raiding party, or west to England and the settlements there. I was open to just about anything, but figured the earl was about to point me in a direction.

There were about thirty men in the hall. Several were from the boat I arrived on, but the rest were unfamiliar, although some of them I had seen in town the past few days. I sat down and the captain went on to the front and sat with the earl. We spent the next half hour in conversation, about half of which I understood. Over the next day, in talks with others, I found out the rest. Basically, three boats would sail back to the general area where we found the merchant boat. Somewhere along the coast was a large river outlet, and upriver was a fertile area with a large town. One of the four captives from the merchant boat was the son of a prosperous nobleman there. The son had convinced the earl that his father would pay a ransom for his release. The plan was to make contact and sell the son back to his family. As opportunities came up, raiding was allowed. The men seemed ready for another trip. As the discussion finished, it turned into a drinking fest and the food showed up, making everyone happy. The captain came over and motioned for me to follow him. We went up to the earl, and I got my assignment. I was to be the guard for the son, and then for the ransom once paid. Apparently, they needed an excellent fighter with no political affiliation. Later, I would find out that these people, just like every other group I knew, were rife with rivalries and political intrigue. The earl believed one of his rivals would either kill the son to keep him from profiting from a ransom, or rivals would go along on the trip, then take the ransom for themselves. They asked me, although it may have been closer to a demand to go along as the guard. I agreed, the earl was happy, and the drunken party continued through the night.

Two days later, we gathered the men, loaded supplies and sailed away from Sweden on the three boats. To my surprise, we went east. The earl had wanted to throw off anyone that might follow us. He was a cagey fox, because I also found out that we would sail by a rival settlement on the Finnish coast. If the small town was undefended, we would have a raid there. If defended, we would pass it up and then turn back west and south. Two days later, the settlement had twelve boats present, so we abandoned thoughts of raiding and backtracked to get the ransom. We laid up on the shore each night so the going was slow. But less risky. Luckily, there were no storms, but the men were also grumbling because there were not any opportunities for raiding. Other than that, everything was quiet on the boats.

I spent my time with the nobleman's son. His version of old German was close to my old Dutch. I could understand him better than the rest of the crew. Once he found out I was not a Viking, but from the Zuider Zee, he became much friendlier. Also, because he knew I was protecting him from assassination. His name was Klaus, and he said his father was wealthy and would be happy to pay to get him back at any price. But after he told me his story, I was not so sure.

His father and other investors had arranged the trading trip and assigned the son as the father's representative. He was the fifth son of a large family; his father had married twice before, was on his third wife, and kept producing children. The normal trade route for that time of year would have been to travel overland for the first part, then charter a boat for the relatively short distance by water to the intended city. That route minimized both storms and the chance of being intercepted by Vikings. However, instead of that less risky option, the cheap bastard had sent them down the river and then all the way around the lengthy isthmus since he had a perfectly good, if leaky, boat sitting at dock. The nobleman should have known better, or maybe he did and was looking to rid himself of a son. The entire account gave me reason to doubt the nobleman would pay anything for his kid. I said nothing as I didn't want to upset him nor give the men a reason to kill Klaus before we even had the chance to ask for a ransom. My gut told me to set up an escape plan. There was time over the next few days to work on something.

I also realized from our talks that the area he was from was Treva. I had not traveled there before but I had heard of it. The town was on a river, where it changed from a large waterway to a series of braided streams. That area was now a prosperous region on the river Elbe and known as Hamburg. The son's description of the intended destination led me to believe he was originally being sent to Copenhagen. Ironic that the old Copenhagen was also a Viking stronghold. The kid was being set up, regardless. He was getting happier the closer we got to his home, while I was getting more worried. I decided I needed a plan to get him home safe, even if the ransom never materialized.

We continued sailing south. By midday, we were in a bay and could no longer sail south as the coastline turned west. From the bay, we entered the mouth of the river and continued for two hours. Then we beached the boats to begin preparations for the ransom demand. One boat would continue up the river to the town and deliver a message that the nobleman's son was alive and downriver. If he paid a ransom of the son's weight in gold, we would put him ashore at the edge of town unharmed. If they did not make payment in three days, then we would send his body ashore instead. Two of our men spoke passable old German, so we chose them to go on the boat and deliver the message. I was glad they were on a different boat and had not heard our conversations. The boat left and went upriver. I stayed on shore with Klaus and enjoyed the day doing nothing.

Three hours later, the boat was back. Message delivered as the two had yelled the demands at the town across the water. Our men were stirred up at the possibility of action or getting paid. I believe most of them hoped for both. Meanwhile, I let Klaus roam on the river shoreline, and I followed him around in conversation, nominally guarding him.

"Klaus, we should prepare for your escape in case things don't go well," I told him.

"Why?" he asked. "My father will have the payment in three days and you warriors will let me go."

Ah, youth. Optimistic unto death.

"Well, things could happen between now and then. What if your father is not even here to raise the ransom? What if he takes longer than three days to find enough gold? Or the Vikings could decide it isn't enough and demand more. We should have a backup plan just in case."

"Yes, I suppose those things could happen. What do you think would work?"

"Do you know how to swim?" I asked.

"Not really. We thought the river was too dangerous for swimming."

"Then how long can you hold your breath?"

I told Klaus what I was planning. If he could hold his breath, I could swim while pulling him long and get us both away from the Viking boat. Then, if we could stay out of range of the archers, I could get both of us ashore, and then him to his father.

I decided we should practice since we were on the river. We waded out into the water, then I coached him to take a few breaths, and then hold the last one. Then I grabbed him and swam underwater, pulling him along. With my physical adaptations and going downriver with the current, we could go a hundred meters before he needed to breathe. We could only get sixty meters against the current. Depending on how the boats formed up on ransom day, this just might work.

Chapter Six

Viking III

The next two days passed slowly. They sent a boat up each of the first two days, but there was no response from the town. The men were getting restless. On the third day, the captain from my first Viking ship came to tell me the plans. All three boats would sail upriver to the town, but two would stay downriver just out of sight of the town. Klaus and I would be on the third boat that would anchor by the town. We would stand at the front so the townspeople could see him. If there was a pile of ransom, our men would retrieve it. Once done, I would toss Klaus into the shallows near the bank and we would depart. If there was no tribute paid, I was to hack Klaus up and throw his body into the shallows. Then the other two boats would land and try to flank the town while we kept their attention.

If all went well, and they paid the ransom, then it should work out easily. If not, I could grab Klaus and dive off the boat and get him to land, since the other two boats would be well out of archery range. I gave Klaus the basic plans and told him that either way he should be back home by the evening.

We got on the boats around noon and headed upriver. Just before town, the other boats fell back as we continued. Klaus and I went to the front of the boat. As we approached town, we saw a wagon with a cover placed near the outside the town wall and fairly near the waterfront. The wagon was at least far enough from town that it was mostly out of range of bows. It looked like something shiny was showing where the cover did not quite extend to the wagon's side. We dropped anchor and four men went to retrieve the wagon and bring it closer to the water to be unloaded.

"I told you he would pay the ransom," Klaus said.

"We will see," I said. Our four men cautiously approached the wagon, keeping their eyes on the town wall.

"Klaus, start breathing and get ready to jump," I said.

He looked at me skeptically, but had the sense to start his breathing. As the men reached the wagon, they pulled the cover off. Six men in armor hiding in the wagon unloaded their cross-bows into our men. Six bolts went into three of ours and they all went down immediately. The fourth man was unscathed some-how, so he swung his sword and took out two men in the wagon before they could defend themselves. Flaming arrows came up from the back end of our boat to signal the other two boats to land and attack. The men on our boat readied for battle.

"Alright Klaus, time to exit this battle," I told him as we went off the boat and into the water.

I swam, pulling him along quickly back under the boat and then to the stern, where we could wait for a moment hidden near the rudder. We came up, and I whispered to him to get ready for a long swim under water. We went back under and I swam down-river fast and as long as I thought he could hold his breath. A hundred meters from the boat and near the bank, we surfaced. The other two boats were not in sight, but they could have unloaded their warriors on the bank just downriver from us.

I pointed to a corner of the town wall and said, "Klaus, we are going to run as fast as possible toward the corner of the town wall I'm pointing to. Before we get there, we are going to split up. You keep going, then stop, raise your hands, and yell out who you are.

That should keep the soldiers in town from shooting you. Meanwhile, I am going to stay hidden in those woods to the side until all this is over. Once the Vikings leave, I will sneak into town, change clothes, and come find you."

He nodded, and we took off running. I then veered into the woods, well out of crossbow range. Klaus stopped soon after, put his arms over his head, and began yelling. I looked back, and the men were not off the first boat yet, and still no sign of the other two boats. Klaus was still safe and almost home.

I saw movement at the top of the wall as several soldiers gathered there. One left as the others stood there. Shortly, an older gentleman appeared and looked down. Klaus waved at him. A few seconds later, three crossbow bolts sped down, knocking him flat instantly. He did not move. The older man left. I guess his father liked him even less than I imagined. I began thinking the old man might need a lesson in manners before I left town.

I moved further back into the woods, then turned inland and jogged away from the river. After a few minutes, I stopped and listened. A group of men were moving between me and the river, toward town. I guess the men from the other two boats had arrived. I climbed a tree and watched as the men from the first boat made a few sorties toward the town gate. There was heavy crossbow and archery fire from the walls, so they stopped short each time and kept their shields up. The second group in the woods had a good chance of making it in town by surprise, but could see from my perch that the other gates were closed and guarded. I did not think three boats of men were enough to take the town. I watched as the men in the trees headed for a side gate. A brief but intense arrow exchange followed. Several men on the walls took hits, but replacements filled their spots. The men on the ground were also taking causalities and they could not climb the gate.

A portion of the men at the back of the crowd broke off and went running to the next gate. They met the same fate as before;

the blocked gate and a hail of arrows and bolts persuaded them to move on. I gave this battle another fifteen minutes before the guys on the ground gave up and went back to the boats. I was five minutes off; the men retreated less than ten minutes later. They trotted back to the woods as they were probably expecting a counterattack, but none came. Once in the woods, the defeat was clear as they slowly slunk back toward the boats. Meanwhile, the attack from the first boat had ended as well, and they were already boarding. Klaus' body had gone unnoticed by the Vikings. They would probably think that both of us were dead somewhere on the battlefield.

I settled into the woods to wait until the Viking boats had left. I needed to get into town, but could wait until things were quieter. A few hours later, a contingent of troops came out of the gate nearest to where I was and moved into the trees and then the river. Two hours later, at dark, they returned. Since there was no sound of battle, the Vikings must have departed.

I waited until the middle of the night, then went over the wall. I found a stable and went up to the loft to spend the night and the following day. Staying hidden was easy as all the men guarded the walls, and scouts were going out on foot without horses. I imagined that the townspeople would tire of this in another day or so. But paranoia was necessary as Vikings had obliterated the town once before.

I was getting hungry, so that evening I went out and stole food. I also borrowed some clothes so I would fit in better when I starting walking around once martial law was over. With the clothes and no weapons, I should look like a resident. I had two purposes; to find Klaus' father and then find transport away from here and toward the west. Neither of those were to be.

The following day, I began profusely sweating. I stayed hidden and hoped this was a passing illness, although I knew it wasn't. Two more days of sweating and fever, then the headache began. I needed to find a place to collapse and sleep for a few years. Luckily, Charlemagne had already been in the area building his Holy Roman Empire. St. Mary's Church, complete with stone crypts, was nearby.

I went to the church and found a promising family crypt on the grounds. It was relatively new, but already had four bodies interned in stone vaults. To my good fortune, they had been there long enough that, when I opened the oldest crypt, only bones remained. I crawled in and pulled the stone cover back into place. Home sweet home, at least for a while. I was Rip-Van-Winkling again.

I regretted not paying Klaus' father a visit, as I knew he would be dead before I woke up. I planned to leave the country and try to move back west. Then I could stay there or try adventures elsewhere, but I had had enough of Germany.

The stone cover being removed from the vault in which I had hidden awakened me. I was groggy but saw the face of the teenager clearly enough as it registered surprise, then horror. And I could hear him screaming as he ran away. I grabbed my sword and wallet and leapt out of the vault. Outside of the crypt building, I could see it was evening. I faded into the shadows. It was easy because there were lots of crypts now, and the church was much larger and looked different. Then as I jogged away, I noticed the clothes I had on were now rags that were falling apart. Time for a new wardrobe.

I stayed for a while at the edge of the churchyard grown large, as the church was now a cathedral. Things had changed a bit during my sleep. The cathedral looked almost finished and was the tallest building around. But outside the yard were other buildings now. The town was a city. This was good because nobody would know me, but bad if they didn't accept my currency, at least until I could steal some. Having gone through this several times before, I knew how to get that easily enough. Clothes were my first necessity. I jumped the low wall and walked into the middle of the city, staying in shadows as much as possible.

Within an hour, I had new clothes and some pocket money, courtesy of a gentleman that was now sleeping peacefully in an alley. I left him some outdated gold coins, so it was not a complete theft; but definitely an assault. I chose him because I thought he was close to my size, but the clothes were snug. Once again, I had grown while sleeping.

I found my way toward the river and an inn, where I ordered some food and a room for the evening. I also paid for a bath. It seemed wise after what must have been a century in a crypt. I ate three dinners that evening, then went up for my bath. It was quite refreshing. I then went back downstairs to listen to conversations while nursing an ale. I needed to know what the environment was like; what year it was, what season it was, were there any wars, were trade ships moving to the west. Worst case was I knew I could walk back to old Holland, but that would be a month, I calculated.

During the evening, I determined I had been out for a century at least; it was late spring; no wars of consequence involved the town, just the unending squabbling common to the region; and ships were traveling regularly, both west and east. I walked back upstairs to plan my next moves. The next morning, I went to the waterfront to look for ships and berths. There were several options, but at each boat I was told to come back tomorrow after the event. When I asked about the event, they directed me to go back to the city center near the cathedral to see the wheel. All the captains and most of the crews were there, so I would not get any answers this day. I wandered back toward the city center, along with many other people. Where I got to witness a disgusting and miserable sight.

There was a mass of people ahead of me, so I hopped up to a roof above a balcony. A man was tied spreadeagled in the heart of the square. A brute was carrying something that looked like a modified wagon wheel. I could not imagine where this was going. Unfortunately, I found out. After lots of teasing with the crowd, the big fellow lifted the wheel above his head and slammed it down on the lower leg of the man tied on the ground. I could hear the crunch from where I was, then the scream from the wounded man. Then damned if he didn't drop the wheel's edge again on the same leg, but a little higher. I could guess this would go on for hours, so I dropped off the roof and went in search of provisions for my upcoming trip.

Most of the shops were closed. I suppose nobody wanted to miss the spectacle. This was the pre-runner for social media and reality television. I found and bought a few things and kept walking to stay out of the square. I could still hear the taunts from the big fellow and the response from the crowd. Occasional cheers went up as another bone snapped. About three hours later, I went back through the square on the way to the waterfront. Most of the crowd had dispersed, so I was a lot closer to the previous action. The wheel was now sitting suspended on a post, and the man, previously tied to the ground, was now woven into the wheel. They had braided all the bonelessly limp limbs through the wheel spokes. I still don't eat soft pretzels because of that image.

In my broken language, I asked a man in the crowd what was next. He said they would keep the criminal on that wheel until death, today or tomorrow, then the body would remain to feed the crows. I asked what his crime was. He was a known thief, was the reply, and he had stolen a bag from an important woman at the market to earn this death. I was definitely ready to leave Germany.

I went straight back to the waterfront and talked my way onto the first boat I could get on that was going west. The crew on the small merchant boat told me it was sailing to Amstel in the IJssel area. Good enough for me. My Viking days were over and I was sailing back to Holland.

Much later I learned from Kal that I had seen Odin on that adventure. He was the old man on top of the city wall that I thought was Klaus' father. Klaus seemed to recognize him so Odin was likely in disguise. Klaus had needed to die that day and Odin had seen to it. The reasons were convoluted but his death prevented a greater evil hundreds of years later. It was another lesson of how small changes in the flow of time could change major portions of the future. And it was dangerous to consider going back and changing anything, even for good reasons.

Chapter Seven

Club Med

I spent some time sailing around the Mediterranean with my great friend Asif during a period when many others were fighting over lands and alleged treasure in the Middle East. We first met there, on opposite sides of one of the many small battles in the area, but quickly resolved our differences and vowed thereafter to not get into other people's conflicts. We began sailing together along with a good crew, for a decade of trade, travel, and adventure.

Merchant boats sailed and were tolerated throughout harbors in the Mediterranean because they were the bearer of needed goods, the basis of building wealth for some, and the source of news and information. What happened in Europe, West Asia, the Middle East, and North Africa traveled by ship much more so than by land. Recently, there were even tidings from China and India. A very early and slow internet of sorts.

Along with that information flow came those intent on using the information for political purposes. Anytime we took on passengers we assumed some were spies for the multitude of nations, cities, independent states, and fledgling empires of the region. We probably took on more than our share compared to other boats as we had a reputation for staying out of conflicts and protecting our cargo better than most. There was also some notoriety as our boat was co-captained by a Christian and a Muslim. Neither of us was actually either of those religions, but we perpetuated that facade as it helped us get into and out of ports that were closed to others. We studied the ever-changing politics and had spy sources of our own. We realized there were lots of opportunities in this sea, what with Africans, Russian Vikings, Italians, Egyptians, Portuguese, Spanish, Lebanese, Cretes, Turks, Franks, Frankish Outremers, and Chinese sailing the waters. And a few dozen other races, cultures, nationalities, and pirates of every sort. Over time, Asif and I had met and cultivated what was more than a friendship with two sisters in Messina, Sicily. It was professional at first since they operated a significant information web and were likely spies themselves. The friendship progressed to more, but all four of us were aware of the conflicts of interest, so we kept business and personal issues separate on the several stops we made at Messina each year.

Meanwhile, our time traveling the seas and visiting the other ports passed quickly. We had plenty of trade to occupy our time, and every trip was an adventure in some way. It did not last, as most things in life ebb and flow. I didn't know it for centuries, but meeting Asif saved my life many times over. Once again, someone I met by chance ended up being one of the most important people in my life.

During our fifth year, seemingly by accident we entered what became a profitable business for ferrying various passengers with specific agendas. Our passengers considered our boat as a neutral territory and very convenient for negotiations. We began picking up passengers that were much more interesting than before. Some trips we spent sailing along the coastline, with no cargo other than passengers that were negotiating for whatever their cause. Soon we also began more official "diplomatic retreat" or "diplomatic tourism" trips, taking groups out to sea, then dropping off most of our crew at a pre-chosen port. The remaining crew sailed us to a nearby uninhabited island. Tents were pitched for the guests while the crew spent their days fishing or lazing on a paid vacation. A lot of diplomatic business was conducted on those jaunts as well as a lot of socialization, as guests began bringing additional guests for entertainment. Ostensibly those were prostitutes, but we noticed via mannerisms that they too were spies. Tangled webs were cast everywhere.

Asif and I were trusted to a great extent by the entities that did business around the sea. Lots of money was traded for treaties with allies that rarely lasted months, and we made sure nothing happened to those funds. We also knew how to be discreet and when to make ourselves scarce. Some things we did not need or want to know. Even so, we had a few incidents where thieves tried to rob us, or where assassins came after us to block particularly important negotiations that apparently needed to be kept quiet. The thieves ended up stranded on a distant island and the assassins found their peace floating face down in the endless sea.

One trip we laughed at for years began as a normal jaunt with four passengers needing quick and quiet passage to Cyprus. Although it took a bizarre turn, the trip did illustrate the cosmopolitan nature of the Mediterranean as well as some of the political intrigues always stewing. During the voyage, at one port we found a new incense from the Orient that was recommended by a merchant we knew. He told us we would enjoy the smoke, so we bought it from his stall in a port near Venice.

Two nights later we added it to all the incense burners in the cabin, mixed with another incense. Asif and I had tried it before and put it in a burner and lit it as instructed. It had an unusual smell but went well with the other types of incense we used to tamp down the occasional pungent smell of the boat. As our guests came in, we served them drinks of their choice, or at least their choice of what we had in stock. Wine, bad ale, or a strong distilled alcohol mixed with lemons was available on that trip.

As usual we began a dice game after dinner. About ten minutes later we noticed our guests acting strangely. The nun superior from Constantinople ended up removing her habit – to reveal a him. He volunteered that he was a eunuch and had been acting as a nun to spy on Rome while a liaison there. He was good at being a nun since his father was a priest. Meanwhile on this trip he was smuggling scrolls stolen in Constantinople to a buyer in Cyprus. Everyone but Asif and I laughed uproariously at the revelation. He and I just looked at each other and wondered why he revealed his secret. And why was it so funny to the other passengers?

The bishop from Rome then joined in the fun to tell us he was actually a Templar from France. He was traveling to Antioch to assassinate a wealthy merchant that had insulted and cheated his patron. That drew more laughter from the other three guests.

The Venetian with the doge's office claimed he was really from the doge's office, but the doge wasn't the doge – he had been replaced twice, the second time by his sister and nobody realized it. He was going to Cyprus to find a body double of the doge to act as a diversion for what they knew was an upcoming assassination plot. But it did not matter whether the doge stand-in was killed or the new body double, just as long as one survived. The Venetians did not want to go through the trouble of finding another real doge as it was too much trouble. Again, laughter.

Finally, the merchant from Jerusalem provided the strangest twist. He was an assassin from Antioch and was on his way back from France after killing a high-ranking Templar that had an enemy in Antioch. He and the Templar rolled around laughing at that absurd coincidence, then became fast friends, at least for the evening.

Just for fun and to join the oddfest, I boasted that I was actually a Roman soldier from Gaul, bringing jeers and more laughter from the passengers. Asif added that his family were architects that helped to build the pyramids. Even louder jeers and laughter descended upon him.

Then things got really weird. The dice game was mellow but became competitive. The four guests began gambling whatever they had, which eventually devolved to their clothing. An hour later they were all mostly unclothed, or I suppose they were, because Asif and I had left them to go on deck. We were afraid that whatever had infected the guests might be contagious. Later we saw then stagger-float out of the cabin and go to their respective hammocks. They appeared extremely drunk but had not finished off more than two drinks each.

The next day we sighted Cyprus. The guests were all very polite to each other but otherwise quiet, almost as if they had hangovers. We were happy to get them off the boat and sail back to the west.

Before we left the docks, though, we solved the mystery of our guests' behavior. A sailor walking past our boat turned around and asked if we had more opium, as he thought he smelled it. I said we did, and he offered to buy it. When I asked what he wanted the incense for, he described the effects it had on him. It certainly explained a lot that had happened. I also realized that Asif and I were immune. I sold some to him and kept the rest on a safe place on the boat. We bought more when we could and kept it on the boat, knowing there would be times in the future when we could use it to great effect. We may need to quell aggressive passengers or ply knowledge from some of the highly placed spies.

Another trip we picked up several important people at a small island off the coast of Italy. We could not depart from a port as the factions the passengers represented could not be seen getting on a boat together. They all made their way to the island, now known as Zannone then boarded our boat. We sailed on to our usual island. There we unloaded and had a pleasant evening as everyone behaved.

The next day three ships appeared on the horizon. Our

lookout spotted them while they were still hours away. Apparently, the secrecy protocols we used had not been enough. Whether one of our two parties had contracted a hit on the other, or this was a third party interested in killing both our groups of passengers, we needed quick action. Asif and I conferred on options.

"We can handle three boats on our own, or at least we could if we hadn't left half our men in port," I said. "But not only are the passengers useless if we fight, we cannot afford to have them injured or drowned."

"Then we run," Asif said.

"Yep, we run."

"Where to?"

"Sicily, to the sisters. It is a big island, plus they have a large estate, connections to hide us, or if needed, enough men to protect us against a large force."

"Plus, we are overdue for a visit. Let us be off."

Everything but a few days of food and water was abandoned on the island. Thirty minutes later we raised sail and began the race. Even with an undermanned crew we made good time and kept leagues between us and our followers. They did not even slow as they passed the island to raid the unoccupied camp, so it confirmed they were after us rather than opportunistic pirates.

Another day and we approached the port of Messina in Sicily. We ported quickly as the harbormaster knew us. It took ten minutes to unload the boat and buy a group of guards to watch our empty boat, just in case our pursuers were mad at us or wanted to prevent us from leaving. The crew filtered into town with orders to act as normal sailors in port but be ready to leave when signaled. Our passengers complained but we cut them into small groups, made then wear head and face coverings so they would not be recognized, and walk through the warm and dusty streets to the estate. Poor things, it was more exercise than some had had in years.

The sisters were entrepreneurial as they were on the diplomatic payroll of a dozen city-states, countries, or provinces. Which meant they were spies, ambassadors, or both. Asif and I knew one of the sisters were working for the Franks, and the other for Malta. Both occasionally worked for Venice or Genoa, whichever paid better that month. In Sicily they were under the protection of the Norman king. There were many others willing to pay for information, including the Muslim areas of Alexandria, Tunis, and Tripoli, the Greeks, Constantinople, and a dozen other factions. It was a lucrative business punctuated by frequent assassinations if the wrong word got out. Which was asinine since everyone in the business already knew all the secrets. Many of the killings were a result of buyers not wanting to pay or cover themselves if something went wrong. A few information mongers, like the sisters, were simply too valuable to kill off. They brokered most of the secrets that went through the Mediterranean.

Marinda and Isandra were waiting for our parties at their gate. A courier had been sent ahead of us. They warmly greeted us and politely greeted our passengers as guests. I could tell both sisters were sizing up the new arrivals up and categorizing them as to their worth in information. The games would soon begin. We'd not told the passengers who the sisters were or what they did. Our passenger's plans were about to become a well-known secret, and the sisters would rake in the money for telling their various bosses.

Guards were posted around the estate to ensure privacy and safety. The guests were put up in immaculate quarters in the estate's main house. Asif and I took one of the smaller homes in a more private location where the sisters could visit. We had a most pleasant week and even spent a few hours making escape plans. We did not have to take responsibility for our passenger's safety but felt it our professional responsibility to get them back home.

Too soon it was time to rouse ourselves from the pleasant situation. The sisters sent messages to our crew in town. They filtered out of the bars and whorehouses to the boat. Some carried supplies, ensuring the enemy sailors at the port were on full alert to an imminent departure. The enemy commander was left with a difficult decision on whether to follow our boat with all of his, knowing Asif, me and the important passengers were not on it, staying in port, or splitting his forces. We had planned on his sending one boat to follow our boat, which is what happened. Meanwhile the sisters had sent two of their boats out the previous day and they were waiting to ambush the enemy boat. It was a quick fight as the sisters could afford the best boats and best fighters. Now we had to make our escape and rendezvous with our ship.

The passengers were dressed as peasants and sent off in pairs. Asif and I were well known in the area so needed better disguises. The sisters dressed us in their servants' clothes, and off we went as large, ugly women with faces partially veiled. Few people are as invisible as ugly servants. It would not pass close scrutiny, but we just needed to get to where we needed to be at night, so it might work. Otherwise, it could be a small slaughter for us to cut our way through guards, most of whom were hired locals.

Our destination was a small harborage outside of Messina exclusive to the wealthy residents in the area. Our opponent had put a guard on it, but obviously they did not think we would sail a smaller boat from there as the main body of guards stayed in the main port. As we approached, we each picked up a sack to carry to the designated boat. The passengers and a small crew had arrived a few hours before and were already aboard. The two closest guards did not even spend a second looking at us or whistling. I should have been insulted. Truly good-looking people transcend gender, but the guards did not see me as attractive either way. We boarded and slipped away from the harbor. We went north along the strait, turned west off the tip of Sicily and met our boat. Back on board our ship we sailed back to Zannone and dropped the passengers.

They had been gone several days longer than expected, but

the quarters were so nice in Sicily they did not seem to mind. The sisters had fully interrogated them in such a nice way they didn't know it even happened. After all the drama, the two parties had resolved the main issue of discussion. Joanna, sister of Richard the Lionheart, was to be betrothed to William, the Norman King of Sicily.

Chapter Eight

Michael

My recent career change had left me somewhat at a loss, since I was working with a completely new set of people. Moving from Alexandria to Italy and changing allegiances from Islam to Christianity had its drawbacks. But I knew I had centuries to adapt and learn all the nuances common to my field before I changed again. Of course, I was neither a proper Muslim nor Christian, as I predated those religions by millennia, but they need not know that. Religions tended to come and go, and few lasted more than two thousand years. My new employer should be good for another thousand years. I rarely worried about it since this was my fifth religious affiliation.

I was in Venice to discuss trade and influence issues between their political empire and the Church. Mostly that meant trading information and gossip about the hundreds of monarchs infesting Europe. Both sides trafficked in any information that could gain us advantages over that raucous bunch, without giving up too many of our own secrets. I also needed to negotiate the release of a merchant arrested in Venice for being a Church operative. Of course, he was, and both sides knew it, but we needed to play out the dance and act as if he was not working for us. The Doge obviously wanted concessions that we both knew I'd eventually give.

Meanwhile we traded gossip over endless dinners and banquets. It was quite tedious but necessary.

The Doge and his followers, the multitude of trade groups that acted as guilds, and the mass of foreign factions, were all drawn here to wealth and power. Venice was one of those early places where capitalism grew out its gnarly roots steeped in the blood of the less fortunate. It was all here in Venice, along with every political intrigue invented by humans. And there were some very inventive humans in this city. A positive byproduct of that system was a relatively open acceptance of peoples and practices not seen in other regions. Peoples of all cultures and religions were welcomed as long as they did business that benefitted Venice. Jews, Greeks, Armenians, Turks, and recently, Mongols and Chinese, maintained residences in the city.

The discussions proceeded without major issues. Ultimately, most of the conversations and deals did not matter; a year later nearly half the people I'd met would be dead from the first wave of the Black Plague. A terrible loss that society could not bear to have repeated. Yet it did, several more times. The human world progresses, and societies grow slowly, then violent change flings them into chaos with unpredictable outcomes.

A few weeks into the byzantine negotiations, I stepped out of an ornate mansion and into a chilly but clear evening. Slightly humid, but then Venice was always humid. A flurry of crossbow bolts whistled through the darkness. I was expecting an ambush attempt as that was typical of a stay in Venice. I dodged most of the bolts, although four hit me and the glass bulb heads broke open as they penetrated my skin. At least two different poisons were now in my body. That explained the unusual whistling sound, as bolts with smaller metal heads made less noise. It was smart of them to try poison.

But not smart enough, as they had no idea wo they were dealing with. The bolts alone would have killed a mortal human, and the poison doubly so. It just annoyed me, as there were now holes in my silk overshirt. To play out the game they expected, I had to let some of the bolts hit, then I had to fall into the canal. Now I was wet and even more annoyed. I swam underwater a few seconds to get a hundred meters away from the site of the attack. I surfaced in the basement of house where a boat was moored. It was in the line of sight of where I went into the water. I stuck my head out and watched several crossbowmen grab poles and slide them into the water to locate my body. There were also a few watchers in boats and basements of nearby houses, so they had cast a wide net.

Ten minutes later the pole wielders gave up, believing my body to have sunk or moved away in the slight current. The group of crossbowmen and the watchers congregated together along the canal for a brief discussion. Then they broke into four groups and moved off in the same general direction along the canals and alleys. I chose the nearest and followed.

After crossing five canals they stopped at a typical house befitting a wealthy owner. They entered but did not come out. Over another half hour, three other groups carrying crossbows entered the house. An hour later, an opulently dressed man wearing a mask, surrounded by men dressed in black silk left the house. It was Carnevale season after all. The men moved oddly, and while watching them I realized it was the first time I had seen a Chinese master vampire and his contingent. Venice had just gotten even more interesting. And I knew the crossbowmen would not ever come out since they had probably been served for dinner. It was likely a smorgasbord of blood and raw meat in there.

The group moved for half an hour in the general direction of St. Marks. Most humans could not discern the true nature of the creatures, but the few humans along the way naturally shied away from the vampires. There must be something hardwired into prey that predators are nearby. The group entered a large building set up as a guild for spices.

There were watchmen, but I easily bypassed them and found

a door on a side alley. I quietly wrenched it open, entered, then propped it closed. The vampires were in discussion with a group even more gaudily dressed than the master vampire. Robes, head scarves, and fancy scimitars, all familiar as I knew these men well.

The Muslim men were my former colleagues. A mix of politicians, bodyguards, and assassins, currently stationed in Damascus. They were obviously under orders to kill me. But they also underestimated me, assuming I was human. Time to disabuse them of that assumption. I calculated the odds, as I needed to kill every man and vampire before the evening ended. But the odds were not currently in my favor. Too many vampires, and too much open space I'd have to cross to get to them. Without surprise, the two groups would have time to scatter, and hunting them down individually would be inefficient. I needed to make a statement with piles of bodies in one place. Since I knew where the vampires were staying, I decided to follow and deal with the other group first.

This was a typical Venetian machination. Nobody wants to take any responsibility if an important emissary from the Church like me goes missing or is found dead and causes political problems for the Doge. He has a squad of assassins that are quite dedicated. That explained why my former colleagues contracted visiting vampires, who then hired out a local gang to kill me. Plausible deniability. In this case, it was just going to get a lot more humans and vampires killed.

I was the primary assassin for the Church, even though it was one of my minor skills. But they did not trust me yet to know their full internal politics, so I was not considered a true diplomat. I knew it would take a long time to earn that trust. Meanwhile I would accept the messenger and negotiation duties, plus rid them and myself of enemies that resorted to martial forms of diplomacy.

Tonight, though, Venice was about to be treated to an orgy of violence. The group of former colleagues made it to a mansion with a warehouse space attached. They went in and bolted the door. Time for the violence to commence.

It was completely unequal of course. My people were designed by those that came before, the ones known as the Makers, that most peoples of Earth would consider gods. They were no such thing, but they did design my people well. I was an example of one of their prototype humans, designed to not age, heal almost instantaneously, and be many times faster and stronger than the humans that came later. We were nearly perfect to watch over and guard humans against their worst instincts, and that became our primary role on this planet. We were few, but most of us were placed in the courts of monarchs or other major organizations, mostly to nudge humans away from their worst impulses.

My innate abilities allowed me to go against my enemies with impunity, but with the knowledge and experience that I'd only kill when other options were not available. Tonight was a rare time that a powerful message needed to be sent. I took a few steps and then leaped through a second-floor window. The scimitars and daggers employed against me never touched me. I had a short knife I always carried, and two minutes later, fourteen bodies bled out into the Persian rugs of the mansion.

Sloppy on one of the neck cuts I had executed, I had a few droplets of blood one sleeve. I didn't bother to stop and wash it off since the shirt already had holes in it and was damp. Likely there would be other stains on the cloth tonight.

The vampire nest would be more challenging, but not by much. They were several times faster than humans and harder to kill. Their speed would not save them. My people had the ability to manipulate time and gravity within our immediate surroundings. I could cast a bubble around me and speed or slow time as needed, and I could change gravity, either to much less or much more than normal. I had never had a fair fight, and never intended to start one.

I strolled up to the front door of the vampire mansion and kicked it in. A good entrance never impresses the bad guys, but I enjoyed it. Two young vampires were on me in a second, then I kept walking as their headless bodies lay twitching. I entered the grand ballroom at the back of the house where I thought the action would be, and I was right. The remains of at least a dozen of the crossbowmen were hanging from ropes as young vampires fed on them. Their master sat in the back with two older vampires. They only ate live meat and looked disgusted at the macabre feast.

I did not want to spook the master and then have to chase him down on the streets or canals, so I let the first wave of outraged vampires nearly touch me. Almost in slow motion I let them near, then barely got my knife up to behead them before they got me. It was tedious and bloody work, and I'd definitely have to throw the shirt away. The next two minutes seemed like hours as I whittled the numbers down. All the young ones were down, and the master seemed slightly surprised. He spoke and the two older ones came at me. Pretenses were no longer needed, so before they took three steps their heads landed on the floor. Now the master looked worried. He stood and made some very good moves. I watched the slow movements from my time bubble, then reached out and removed his head.

The next morning I was back in my Venetian business casual clothing and sitting in one of the largest houses in Venice. The Doge often had morning meetings in this house rather than his office building, which of course was one of the largest buildings in Venice. This house was more comfortable, and also contained more guards per square foot than the office building. He was a cagey character, but long-lived for a reason. We had tea and small sweets for our continuing negotiations, then he led with a different inquiry.

"An unfortunate incident occurred last evening," the Doge

said. "It was said that a demon with supernatural speed killed more than thirty men."

"That seems excessive," I responded.

"Would you know anything about it?"

"I doubt that the Church would employ demons."

He stared at me for a moment then gave a slight nod. It was never mentioned again. In later visits to Venice, I had no further attempts on my life. A week later my work in Venice was done and I arranged passage back home, anxious to see my wife and daughter.

While arranging my trip home I spent time around the docks. I was hoping for any word of a certain missing seafarer. Most everyone in the Mediterranean with a boat eventually docked in Venice. But I learned nothing useful. Still, I spent some money in the taverns talking and drinking with ship captains. I became known among them, and they knew how to reach out to me if they came across the person I was searching for, someone very important to me. Although missing, I knew he was not dead. Yet the presence was faint. It was very odd, and something I'd never encountered before, nor had any of my people ever experienced this feeling. There was nothing I could do but keep searching and spreading the word among those that might have contacts across the seas.

That trip to Venice cemented my role as Chief Protector of Church Interests. It was a fancy term for enforcer and assassin. I performed it as necessary, and continued as a type of ambassador for several more decades. It took another century before a Pope finally trusted me enough to act as a true ambassador. Threats from my former colleagues rapidly diminished after the Venice incident. They turned their eyes to other pursuits in the region, including threats from the Mongols. I also knew that they knew that they couldn't kill me, so it was in their interest to forget me.

Chapter Nine

Pirate

Small name, big deeds. That is an English translation and slight paraphrase of song lyrics written about an old friend. Piet Hein was the most successful pirate in history, even if some have never heard of him. Although he was not a true pirate, but rather a privateer. He was commissioned by the Dutch government to do damage to their enemies on the sea, mostly Spain. Part of the political drama of that era pitted Holland against Spain, so there was usually maritime conflict in both the Old and New Worlds.

The Zilvervloot was the Dutch word for the Spanish silver fleet. The Spanish empire was perfecting the art of looting the Americas. A huge fleet of massive galleons sprouting cannons kept the fleet safe except from storms. Meanwhile every other country dreamed of stealing those riches, but none had the firepower of massed Spanish galleons to take it.

WePiet and I knew each other through the Dutch East India company and later through the Dutch West India company. As a medium-sized investor I knew many of the players, and Piet was both an investor and ship's captain. We had a circle of acquaintances in common, and through them we met. I was interested in his stories of sailing in the East and West Indies as I had not yet made it to either. I learned he hated slavery and governments, having been a Spanish slave a few years and a member of the government of Rotterdam for a year. Both of those dislikes we had in common.

Piet took a trip to the Caribbean as a privateer. Through luck and an excellent spy network, he captured a major portion of the Spanish treasure fleet. Officially there was more than 50 tons of silver, lots of gold, chests of jewels, barrels of the valuable pigments of indigo and cochineal, and other trade goods. No slaves were taken since Piet did not participate in that outrage. And he did not lose a single man, because he was so lucky there was no enemy fire.

Piet was the luckiest man I ever knew. Of course, the pendulum of luck swings between good and bad. He had an abundance of extremely good luck punctuated by bouts of incredibly bad luck. For instance, early on he was captured by the Spanish and forced into slavery. He escaped and began a lucrative career as a ship captain. Then he was then recaptured into Spanish slavery. Once again he escaped, became a most successful businessman, then the most famous pirate in history. But less than a year later he met an untimely end by a stroke of the worst luck.

After capturing the Spanish fleet, Piet was known for his remark that "I'm famous for something that wasn't hard at all, but the things I've done and should be famous for nobody even knows about." His actual quote was much more profane. Leaving out most of the profanity and paraphrasing, his statement was: "I work my ass off to do the right thing for this country, but the only thing they care about is money. All my deeds were ignored until I made them rich by stealing from a Spanish fleet that was too scared to even fire one cannon at me."

Ironically, when he returned to Leiden with ships wallowing in the massive wealth of silver and other treasures, we ended up on a wild goose chase. I visited Piet at his house when invited to a small party. It became raucous to the point of absurdity. His lovely wife was not amused. She told us in no uncertain terms that behavior would not be tolerated in her home. Then she told us our penance. We were to go goose hunting before dawn and not return until we'd learned our manners. Banished to the frigid outdoors, it was still better than disobeying her orders.

Piet wasn't keen on getting out in a boat on a half-frozen marsh before dawn, and neither was I. He was in the throes of a hangover, and I didn't tell him I did not have one. But we had a secret cure, warm milk punch leavened with Caribbean rum and spices. We loaded up some flintlocks, powder, and shot and trudged out to the wagon in what seemed the middle of the night. At least we didn't have to ready the wagon, as Piet had a stable boy prepare it and harness the horse for us. We headed out into the darkness in silence.

"Hey Piet. How's the wife, other than last night?"

"She is happy for me to be home. As am I. Every time I'm home I say I will never sail again. But something always comes up and off I go like an idiot. I'm getting tired of being away."

"You sound sad. I can cheer you up. Say, Piet, what is twelve inches and Dutch?

No idea, what?

"Nothing, absolutely nothing."

"Ha ha. A regular jokester."

"Hey Piet, what is eight inches and Dutch?

"More of this nonsense? I don't know, what?"

"The short leash your wife keeps you on."

"Even more funny. Hey Sen, what is four feet long and loaded?"

"I have a feeling I know, but what, Piet?"

"The guns in the back of this wagon. So, tell your jokes accordingly. If I weigh your body down, it will never be found in the marsh."

"That's more like it. Now you sound like a man ready to go hunting."

We were quiet for awhile in the wagon. It was slow going but we were in no hurry. I sometimes teased Piet about his wife, but he adored her and I knew she was a good person.

"Sen, you really need to find a good woman like I have and settle down. Or rather, let her choose you."

"You are probably right, Piet. Your wife is a good woman. Maybe I'll travel over to the New World and find one someday."

"Hah, good luck with that. The Portuguese, the English, the French, and the damned Spanish are all over there and messing things up. Even the Dutch."

"That sounds interesting."

"Interesting enough to get you killed in the confusion. Beyond all the European nonsense, the natives have many tribes and languages. Every island can be different, and every few leagues along the mainland tribes change. Customs are different so what is a sign of respect in one place will get you tortured to death a half-day voyage away."

"I definitely need to go there."

"Well, you have been warned. I myself tend to stay on the boat when in port to stay out of trouble."

I swear half the milk punch was gone before the wagon stopped at the marsh near a wooden rowboat. It was long, wide, and mostly flat-bottomed skiff with shallow sides. It could not handle rough water but was a typical marsh hunting skiff and very stable. Stable enough to stand up and urinate after all the milk punch. Piet had no problem with me volunteering to handle the oars.

We piled our guns and supplies, the remainder of the milk punch skins, and pushed off into the swirling black water sprinkled with ice falling from the rushes. The winter marsh was starkly beautiful as the dawn progressed. Too early for the wind, we heard every plop and ripple made by whatever was moving out there.

"Hey Piet, since you already are a hero for capturing the silver fleet, are you expecting a golden goose today?"

A few mumbled expletives floated from the other end of the boat. Then silence, but I knew Piet could not resist the jibe.

"You know, I make the officials and people lots of money with dangerous trade, and I get nothing from it, other than how much more can I do for them the next year. I capture and execute pirates, which is really dangerous business, and I get no notice or thanks. Then I float around in calm weather in the tropics, convince an undefended fleet to surrender, and suddenly I'm the most famous Dutchman in the world. But anyone could have done it."

"Yes, but it was not anyone, it was you. And nobody ever brought home fifty tons of silver before."

"Oh, it was a lot more than that. That was the official tally." I could tell from his tone that Piet was finally smiling.

"How so?"

"Before we sailed back, we paid all our men a double bonus. We stopped at several of the Dutch islands and left a small fortune with the directors or governors for future favors. Even when we arrived and before docking in Leiden, another fortune was transferred quietly from our holds to a certain political figure to help him fund his portion of the war outside the government budget. Less than half made the official count."

Even I was surprised. "You are saying that after all that siphonage, you still had fifty tons left?"

"Yes."

"I'm amazed at the audacity. It seems the Spanish would have spoken up at the difference in the official and unofficial amount of plunder."

"They would be the last to make any noise. There is so much graft in their system, even their official manifest only carried fifty tons."

"What, even they siphon off fifty percent of everything meant for their king in Spain?

"Usually more."

"Amazing. No wonder so many of the ambitious make for the New World."

"Mankind's greatest embezzlement scheme so far."

And it was true, at least until America created Wall Street.

It was quiet for a time as we listened to the morning's slow awakening. More distant splashes and bird calls began as our small universe expanded as the light increased. The glow in the east turned into a kaleidoscope of colors just above the shallow fog layer. We set up the boat, loading the flintlocks with powder and shot.

I had already become much less a hunter than in my old days, and only participated in these events for the social aspect. I'd miss more shots than I'd make, but at least on this hunt most of the meat would be to feed a family that Piet knew nearby. They had a need for it as the family's oldest son had become a sailor but had not come home from his latest voyage. The other sons were still too young to add much to the family's income.

A few flocks of geese and ducks flew off the marsh just before dawn, and several other flocks flew in. We made a number of shots and had several birds down and in the boat. By mid-morning the flights had ceased as they normally did, and we were just floating and talking. We went ashore to relieve ourselves and have a snack, then picked up one gun each and got back on the boat and floated out. It was unlikely that any other flocks would come in so late, but we took the guns anyway. Extra shot and powder stayed on shore. The boat slowly drifted into a hummock of dead reeds matted together, some meters from a small island. The sun made an appearance so we laid back in the boat and absorbed sunshine and the last of the liquid warmth from the milk punch, making both of us drowsy.

Loud honking from close overhead got our attention. A small

flock of geese came in and dropped into the water beside the island, not far from where we floated. We carefully and quietly repositioned ourselves and the guns in the boat. With hand signals we made plans to booth shoot at the large gander in the group that was the acting lookout. We rose up and fired together. The small flock flapped across the water to gain altitude to leave the marsh. The gander did not follow, as it was clear one wing hung down limply. One of us had clipped him but not nearly killed him.

"Well, Piet, looks like a goose chase is in order."

He grunted as I put the oars out and started toward the injured bird. He saw us coming and dropped underwater. I moved the boat to near where he went under. Then we played a very slow game of marco polo, as he would surface twenty meters away from where he dived. I'd move the boat toward him, and when we were close, he would dive again, resurfacing two minutes later. We played the game of slow chase for about forty minutes. The gander was getting tired, as he stayed under for shorter and shorter times, and only swam about a few meters before surfacing. There was nothing we could do but chase as we had no powder or shot left, nor did we even have a knife. I was not sure what we'd do if we finally caught him. You can't wring a gander's neck as it is too strong. I could have, but I had no intention of killing it that way nor alerting Piet that I was more than human. Finally, we got lucky as the gander surfaced right by Piet. In a foul mood by now, Piet quickly grabbed the gander by the neck and held him underwater.

I waited a few minutes. Piet was shaking he was so cold from holding his arm under the water.

"Hey Piet, is your arm cold?"

"Of course it is, you idiot."

"Hey Piet, how long can a goose hold its breath underwater?"

"Many minutes?"

"Yeah, I think so. I'm betting you get frostbite before that bird gives up the ghost. On the positive side, think of how much weight you'll quickly lose when we saw that rotten arm off."

He began cursing and lifted the bird out of the water. The gander did not flap much due to the injured wing. Lucky for us, as a wing flap from a healthy gander can easily break a man's wrist. I leaned forward and put a small piece of rope around the gander's neck and looped it around one leg, then tied it to the boat. Neither of us had the desire to kill it, and we had a grudging respect for its toughness. But it would not survive long in the frozen marsh. I rowed us back to shore and we unloaded the boat's contents into the wagon. On the way back to Piet's house we dropped the less lively birds off to the grateful family that was appreciative of birds for dinner. By this point neither Piet nor I had a taste for goose.

And that is the story of how Piet, after a wild goose chase, ended up with a new pet. One that lived in his yard and turned into an excellent watchdog. Piet's wife fed it several times a day and thoughtfully added a few female geese. The feisty old gander ruled that yard for some seven years afterward.

Piet's run of luck continued as usual. But, as in the strange turns his life had taken, this time it was bad luck. Once again doing the right thing for his country, he took his boat after pirates that were sailing out of Dunkirk. They were funded and backed by the Spanish. Early in the battle, a cannonball removed the upper left portion of Piet's body, and he left this world. Despite the long history of cannons in ship warfare, not that many men were killed by a direct hit from a cannonball. It was luck, I suppose. As unlucky as it was for Piet, I also grieved as I lost another friend.

But Piet's legacy did not end. He was never completely forgotten, certainly not in Holland and as it became later, the Netherlands. A couple of hundred years later a song came out about Piet and his exploits, a song that fit nicely into the Dutch habit of singing about their heroes in the taverns. I heard the song as late as

2005 during a rowdy academic dinner held in a castle near Arnhem. Every Dutch person sang along at the top of their voices.

How lucky was Piet to be remembered so fondly hundreds of years after his death? I don't think anyone noticed my tearing up with all the drinking and singing happening. Small name, big deeds. Indeed.

Chapter Ten

Revenge

Greater Europe was a mess. It had been for a while and would continue for several more centuries. Spain, France, England, Portugal, Holland, the Germanic provinces, Sweden, and Russia were all terrible in their unique way. Conquest abroad, subjugation of their own people, and awful mismanagement by the rulers were common traits among them. Superimposed on all that were the regional "managers" of the Holy Roman Habsburgs and the Church. Neither of which was very good at anything. Spain was heavyweight of the bunch but due to financial mismanagement was floundering and everyone else was trying to cash in, especially France. Alliances were formed and broken as soon as the seasons changed. Mankind was doing what came natural whether martial or financial. Everything was a competition toward ultimate greed, and everyone else was evil and deserved to be punished or executed.

France, in the midst of that turmoil, decided to add territories to the north. Not ready to challenge Spain directly, they hopped over the Spanish Dutch provinces, and also swept up through Cologne to invade Holland proper. It was 1672, and once again misery came to the people that were not nobility. It lasted six years, and when finished not much had changed. A similar result of the earlier hundred years war and the eighty years war, and the later second hundred years war. The human rulers were proving there was no disagreement too low to throw the lives of the ruled away for.

The French warmongers had sent the armies north to gain a little territory and of course, fame and wealth for France. Initially very successful for the French side, it bogged down as the Dutch did what they could to hinder the advances. For a small, flat country with no major rivers or other geography to act as barriers, they used their brains to survive. The weapon of choice became water, and what the brilliant engineers did with it. If you invaded Russia, you fought the winter; if you invaded Holland, you fought the water.

Montmorency, Duke of Luxembourg was a hideous little man, literally and figuratively. Foppish yet hunchbacked, he was the worst of the French aristocracy. His deformity made him even more insecure, and therefore crueler than most. A perfect appointee to grind down the Dutch. I began calling him Monty.

On one campaign, a portion of the French army under his direct command decided to give out presents for the holidays. Two days after Christmas, in the middle of winter, his forces marched out to the west to engage the enemy. Dutch forces were not ready to fight, but they able to cut the dikes and sluices in time to stop the advance. Half of the French column was caught in the rising waters. Monty had to turn back and the advance group had to slog through the cold water and retreat. They decided to have a little fun in the way back to their quarters. Stopping at a few villages, including Bodegraven which was a neighbor of Woerden, the villagers were herded into their homes, the doors barricaded, and houses set afire to burn them alive. After a long, cold day outside the fires kept the French soldiers warm. I suppose it also assuaged Monty's hurt feeling that his assault had failed. Since Bodegraven was close to Woerden, I knew some of the people there from market days.

When I heard the news, I was in Amsterdam as I had left Woerden when the French invaded. It was time for me to get involved in the kerfuffle threatening to swallow Holland. The French were just as easy to kill as anyone else, and they deserved to suffer a little.

Killing off a large number of soldiers at one time was not easy. Blowing up a large bridge they were marching across, or the castle or camp they were occupying was possible. But unlikely, as getting them to be still and let me bring in several wagonloads of black powder was difficult. It would be another two centuries before humans perfected the methods best able to kill masses of other humans quickly. I needed other sneakier means to kill a lot of Frenchmen. And give pause to the survivors or encourage them to leave the country.

After some thought, perhaps I could use the French army's tactics against it. As invaders they were confiscating everything they could to make their lives easier in the camps. I commissioned a shipment out of Amsterdam and advertised for two wagons full of cargo destined for Woerden. As expected, I had trouble finding drivers as they knew the shipments would be waylaid and confiscated by the French. I offered double the normal wage and signed a contract to hold them harmless if their cargo was stolen by the French. I told each they should put up no fight and if the wagons were taken, I would leave funds for them in Utrecht to travel back to Amsterdam.

I chose the cargo carefully. Multiple barrels of wine and spirits, other alcohol, and multiple hoops of fine soft cheeses. Assembling the wagons in a warehouse in Amsterdam, I first unwrapped the cheeses and prepared them according to my recipe. A few months previously I had gone around the countryside and picked different types of mushrooms of the *Amanita* genus. They were better known by their common name of deathcap mushrooms. I was studying them and their strangely toxic abilities. I had even tested a few but found they had no effect on me.

I boiled a cauldron of beef broth to reduce it by three-fourths, took it off the fire, then dumped in all the mushrooms. The toxin is heat stable and the hot broth would bring out all the goodness from the dried fungi flesh. I let the concoction sit overnight, strained out the mushrooms, then soaked the soft cheeses in the liquid. Each cheese soaked up a small amount, but it was enough to kill several men. The beef broth covered the acrid taste of the mushrooms. It was a crude but effective way to wipe out an officer corps of an army that dared to steal a shipment destined for Woerden. I then recased the cheeses and loaded them on the wagons for shipping.

I had other preparations to make, and I had to get myself to Woerden before the wagons left Amsterdam. Two days later the wagons left and I began the next phase. As expected, the wagons did not arrive in Amsterdam. Monty's toadies confiscated everything including the wagons. My drivers earned their pay as they had to walk back to Utrecht. I kept a watch on the French camp and saw my wagons taken into the storage building near the officer's quarters. The regular soldiers would never see the good stuff. I expected the wagon's contents to make their way into the officer's mess in a day or two. Phase two began the next morning. I needed to draw as many of the soldiers and officers out the camp as possible and give them a workout. I was not much of a threat as one man, but I had a provocation they could not ignore.

The previous evening, I had taken souvenirs from eight different tents in the camp. This morning I had ambushed a small foraging patrol and taken their heads as well. That gave me a few extra to entice the French to chase me. I had all the heads in my heavy bag as I put them on spikes on the road leading out of the camp in the direction I wanted them to follow.

When the camp noticed what was on the road they sent out a group to scout. I was two kilometers away from the camp by now, so I added those heads to my bag. I ran along the road raised above the marshes and fields, placing French heads on the bare trees that grew along the road about every four hundred meters. Where there were no trees I used the pikes from the soldiers, since they no longer had need of their own weapons.

The camp soon realized that someone had infiltrated the camp and killed their comrades. The earlier patrol also had not returned, so the French smartened up and sent out a much larger force to deal with a substantial threat. This group included cavalry, as I had expected, but by now I was a dozen kilometers away, across a bridge and at the end of a line of severed heads.

Ahead there was a low place on the road. The last two days I had been opening sluices nearby to raise the water above the roadbed. It was shallow but it was enough for my needs. I ran across and continued preparing for my guests, sowing the last of my presents. It was already cold and wet, because it was Holland in the winter. Ugly conditions for humans but not so much for me. I was determined to introduce the worst of Holland's climate personally to every French soldier under Monty's command that I could find. I hoped that and my other gifts would encourage them to leave Holland.

I waited a few hundred meters past the water-covered road, barely in sight of the oncoming soldiers. They approached the shallow water skimmed with ice that covered the road. The troops could see the far side where the road rose up out of the water, and me jogging away with a soldier's head in one hand. It was an easy decision for them to chase me. What they did not know would hurt them.

Caltrops were strewn in the hard mud under the frigid water, along with a few sets of rope ladders from ships that I had staked out a few inches below the surface. I'd also dug some knee-deep post-holes in the roadbed.

The French calvary charged down the road. Then horses screamed and went down hard, men cursed, and water sprayed in gouts as human and equine bodies hit it at high speed and thrashed about. The last men in the charge pulled hard at their horses but even then, momentum flung some of them forward into the traps, or they tripped over the maimed bodies of horses and men in the water, while others went off the side of the road and into the deep and steep-sided canal ditches lining the roadbed. The cavalry group was decimated. I dropped the head where they could see it and ran faster down the road.

It was some distance to my next destination. I knew the survivors would be wary of following me, but their officers would push them ahead. They probably assumed I was a straggler from a larger group. Like human males throughout history, they couldn't not chase after prey.

I got to my position and dropped the next-to-last head in the road. To the right, across a hundred meters of marsh was a wooded island. I waded into the water and swam to it. I put the last head on a branch nearby and waited. The column marched up the road and halted as they picked up the head. I started yelling the few French curses I knew to get their attention. The officers formed the men into a firing line and a volley flew toward me from their flintlocks. Not the most accurate weapon, but there were a lot of them, and they were all aimed at a small spot where I had been standing. Just before the order to fire I had sprinted back into the trees as I didn't want to be exposed to that much lead. I figured they would wait until the smoke cleared, then send scouts over to look for my body.

By then I had crossed the island and was rowing my small boat hard down the channel back in the direction of the camp, but a kilometer away from the road. I only stopped to open every sluice I passed. The last stop was the bridge we had crossed earlier. Two barrels of stolen black powder were strapped to the main supports. I lit the long fuse and kept rowing. Moments later I heard the explosion. I landed the boat on a spot of dry ground and jogged to another wooded area and mounted the horse I had tied up there. I rode him to a few kilometers from the camp, then waited in a dry spot.

Blowing up the last bridge had given me plenty of time to get back to the camp before the men and officers arrived. They were still in the middle of a long, tedious, and unrewarded day chasing me. I knew the soldiers and officers would end up slogging through the water and mud rather than stopping for hours to rebuild the bridge even if they had the materials to do so. I had plenty of time to rest and think through the final step.

The camp after the day's events was watchful but also under-manned. As night fell and before the small army made it back to camp after chasing me, I entered camp and broke into the storage area. Most of my barrels were still there, but one barrel of wine and one of brandy were gone. The cheeses were still stored undisturbed. Good, the plan was proceeding. I found the two barrels marked with a black X and tapped the first and began draining it into a bucket. I opened the barrels of wine and spirits and drained a liter or two from each into the floor drain. I refilled each of them with the contents from the bucket using a funnel, then replugged each with the bung. I continued until most of the contents of both marked barrels were gone, then poured the rest down the drain.

I did not touch every barrel so if they suspected contamination, they would not easily find it. But now most of the barrels had a healthy dose of wood alcohol. It was untraceable as there was no denaturant added to make it unpalatable.

Men affected by wood alcohol poisoning would show initial signs of inebriation, followed the next day by what appeared to be a bad hangover, or possibly food poisoning. After that, muscle failure and blindness, the irreversible stages of the poison, would likely alert the camp medics of the origin of the illness. I hoped by then quite a few of the men would be in the later stages, with death soon after.

About a day after eating the cheese, the men would exhibit symptoms of food poisoning. An army camp always had poor rations so the bouts of illness would be unremarkable enough to not arouse suspicion. The men would recover a day or two later and go about their duties. A week later their livers would slough off into fatty jelly, their kidneys would fail, and they would die in a few hours. Even if the commanders did figure out it was mushroom poisoning, death caps were common to area, so the cause could be from a foraging mistake. I doubted they would ever suspect the cheese.

My work in the camp was done and I crept out. All I needed to do was wait in Woerden for a week and watch from a distance as many of the officers were either buried on site or wrapped up for a wagon ride back to France. It was going to be a terrible ride for the drivers. The liquified insides of the bodies from those killed by the cheese would drain out orifices for some time, possibly all the way back to France. Even in the middle of winter the wagons would be a mess of putrefied livers and kidneys. I thought it an appropriate end for those that had torched the families of Bodegraven and other villages during the holidays.

The French soldiers began dropping into illness. A number of them, mostly young officers in the middle ranks from that army did not survive the next two weeks. Unfortunately, Montmorency and his immediate staff had left camp after that first night to meet other leaders for a planning conference, so only one of them succumbed to the mushrooms. But the overall effect was enough to cripple some of the army's operations. The symptoms were so mixed that I don't think they ever figured out exactly what was happening, but they did eventually throw out all food and drink and brought in new supplies from France.

I considered following up with further retribution, but decided the constantly changing allies and battle conditions were best left to William of Orange to deal with. Monty had to beat a hasty retreat soon enough rather than face a much a larger army. His retreat from Holland somehow made him a hero in France. I suppose that is what propaganda does – making lemonade from lemons. But like a bad virus, he kept coming back. He "defeated" William of Orange multiple times, but never decisively enough to put him away. So they kept battling various places. I realized I should have taken care of Monty myself. The lesson from that mistake prompted me to deal directly with German invaders three hundred year later.

Eventually the war, like most, simmered down to the point that even more deals were made. Papers were drawn, courtesies extended, and all the soldiers and peasant victims long since buried. And the war ended, until the next one began over reasons just as stupid as the previous one.

France could have gotten almost all of Holland if they had been slightly more aggressive the first year or taken the original peace deal and gotten half of Holland. But they persisted in dreams of battle and glory, and eventually got little for the effort. Yet once again the fops did well, and everyone else suffered. Humans were not very good at learning lessons. At least not those at a high enough level to avoid suffering.

Chapter Eleven

Gift

My time in colonial America was, up to that time, the happiest two decades of my life. Finding a true mate, building a home with a flourishing family, and staying out of conflicts was a dream. It was my time of magic. But if you live long enough you find that dreams and magic can end as fast as they come.

During our time in Brasstown Valley, we always made time to explore. The kids liked to hike to the ridgeline nearest us to the west. Some of the caves we found there had been visited before, perhaps even lived in seasonally. Blackened floor near the entrance indicated hearth fires, and there were drawings and carvings on the walls and ceilings. We made sure not to disturb any of those. Birds, animals, spiders, and other odd characters that looked like space aliens were scratched or painted everywhere. I was not to see those again for a few hundred years, but somehow the drawings were a view of both the past and the future.

One summer passed quickly, and I wished I had known it was our last summer there. Hia had decided we needed to move north to a large village of her adopted people. I realize now she knew more about fate and time than I did, and it was necessary for what was to come.

We made all the preparations for the move. One of the last days there we hiked to the caves. In our favorite cave, each of us left a small memento to mark our visit, then my children and I sealed up the entrance to the cave. We pulled a slab over it then replanted some brush to hide the entrance to keep any animals or curious humans out.

The journey to Cowee Town in the early fall was quite pleasant. On the journey, Hia had news for me.

"Sen, you need to know that I left something for you in the cave," she said.

"What is it? Something we need soon?"

"It is very important, but you should not worry yourself about it for a very long time."

"OK, I'll not think about it." I assumed it was a trinket like those we often gave each other, such as small gold nuggets from the creek or crystals from the mountainside.

"Good. We'll talk more about it when the time is right."

We continued the pleasant march to our new home. For a few years we had a good life there. Then a series of events brought that to an end. Our eldest son had gone out to live his life and gotten caught up in the Regulator rebellion against the British Governor Tryon in North Carolina. As a leader he was one of a few that was hung for his actions. But that was only one of the problems that the British government and white settlers were causing for us. Land encroachment, shady deals, and skirmishes that resulted were all too common across the region.

After we heard news of our oldest son's death, we made plans to gather all our family together. Hia also sensed from her Nunehi heritage that the Cherokee people as well as all the Nunehi needed to discuss the problem of white encroachment. Despite her grief she began preparations for a larger gathering.

The gathering for our family together took some days as the older children were spread out with their own families. Messages were also sent to begin the Nunehi gathering. That had not been done for many years. The meeting would be in Cowee, which was not central to the widely spread population of Nunehi, but was easy travel for most of them.

The invited began arriving over the next two weeks until there were thirty-two besides our family. Some had not come because of obligations elsewhere, and a few had not been contacted because they had disappeared. Whether they were on journeys or dead in the wilderness was unknown. It was unlikely that they were dead, however. When shifters passed away, the others usually felt their absence. It was possible they had decided not to attend so they would not be bound by any decisions made.

The Cowee residents were curious about all the newcomers, but recognized them, and generally left us alone except to say kind words in passing and offer food each day. It was beginning to feel like a Council of Nicaea, but I hoped we would be better behaved. The gathering became known as the Cowee Council in later years. I attended but had no intention of speaking other than to answer questions.

The group of us, now numbering just over forty, went out to a small meadow by the river to sit and talk. Hia was the host and made introductions and relayed the basis for the gathering. She had seen in visions what was to come, and also that there could be a way forward despite all the heartbreak and obstacles forecast. Surprisingly, nearly half the group had also had very similar visions. Everyone agreed that the next generations would be very difficult for the people.

The more troublesome part was deciding what to do about the visions and ensure the people's survival. They spent much time in discussions with many ideas but no decisions. The next day was was the same, and the discussions continued. A slight majority felt the Nunehi should stay as cohesive as possible and directly guide the people through the troubles for the next ten generations. Others felt that the course should be to continue interactions with the people as per tradition, and to ride out the troubles with no direct intervention.

Several decades later, this split in philosophy would materialize during the decade of the Trail of Tears. The interventionists tended to stay in the East; quite a few stayed mostly in North Carolina. The traditionalists eventually traveled west to Oklahoma in the years immediately after the Trail of Tears. They helped out the people there, even if indirectly. The two groups maintained some occasional contact afterward, but they were not close.

The Council ended the following day with little headway. All attendees had decided that the Nunehi shifters would not take part directly in violent conflicts but continue in roles more akin to that of a shaman or healer. Privately, my family and several interventionists decided to maintain close communications and act as guides for those in need, but still not taking part in battles. In my ignorance, I thought there was plenty of time to plan and prepare for the future troubles.

I had attended the sessions but had not spoken up, nor been asked questions. Hia was the obvious leader and kept the meetings focused and positive. After the last session ended, a few of the eldest shifters spent the night before making the trek to their homes and villages. The eldest of those, Ihlya, ate with us that night. Afterwards, he sat with Hia and me at the fire.

Ihlya looked at Hia. "This is the one spoken of? He looks... interesting. Kind of shiny silver. Very hard. Has something extra, but also lacks something. Most unusual. But you vouch for him?"

"Yes, we have been mates for many years, and I trust him. He is like us, just as strong and fast as we are, but he does not change. But he lives far longer."

"How old are you?" he asked me.

"Even accounting for your long lifespans, I was born about eight of your lifetimes ago."

"You remember all that? Must be difficult to keep up with much stuff in the head."

"Part of that time I was asleep, like a bear in winter but for years. But the times I have been awake, I remember most of it. Lots of good, lots of bad. Lots of life, lots of death."

"If you have been alive that long among the white people from the East, you must know them well. What do you think they will do now that they are here among us?"

"They will keep coming, taking what they want by force or through playing politics among the tribes. Unless you can raise a vast army and fight them for a thousand years, they will take all you have here, and none of the people will be left. My former, the conquerors, did that to empires much larger than yours. Even if you could combine the strength of all the known tribes, we could have conquered that in less than a generation."

He thought for a few minutes. "Then we must fight less, but smarter. We should let them absorb us on the surface, but keep together out of their sight and outlast them. Did any tribes from your world succeed at that?"

"Yes, a few did, and are still viable hundreds of years later. It is wise to do so here if the people cooperate."

"We will try it. Hia, do you agree?"

"Yes, if my husband has seen that it can work then we must try."

"Just two other thoughts from my perspective," I added. "The shifters must always stay hidden. Otherwise, my kind will hunt you relentlessly and kill all. They fear what they do not understand. Also, the different factions of my kind will try to play the tribes against each other. Do not ally yourself to the British, or the French, or the colonists, exclusively. Or at least try to convince the leaders of the people to remain neutral. I know that the people have already aligned themselves with the British but that could be dangerous in the future."

Ihlya nodded agreement. We sat in silence the rest of the

night, contemplating the dangers ahead and the plans that would need to be made. A day later and everyone that had traveled to attend the council was gone. My sense of foreboding was well nourished by future events.

A week after the council Hia took me to walk along the river. It was a familiar walk for us and reminiscent of previous days walking along the creek of our homestead to the south.

"Sen, I must tell you something important. You know who and what I am, but there is also more that I have not told you."

"Will your mysteries never cease?"

"Soon enough. But this you must know. The caves along the ridge near our Brasstown home that we visited often. Before we left, you remember our favorite cave, the one we painted in and left keepsakes similar to the practices of my ancestors?"

"Yes, the one we sealed up to keep others out after we left."

"I was entrusted in this life with a very important item, one that has passed from mother to daughter in my line for hundreds of generations. Just one of its benefits gave me even more healing power than most of my kind. But I left it in the cave for you."

"What? Why would you do that? You should have kept it and used it to help sustain your powers."

"No, it was time to pass it on. Not to our daughters, that time is over, as this world changes to something different. It is there waiting for you, and for our later descendants. When the time is right it will call for you, and for them. Until then it is safe and won't be needed. But the world will be greatly changed, and you and our family will need it."

"I'm not sure I understand fully, but I will wait for the call."

"Yes, and you will know it when it happens. Our distant children will also feel it, so all of you will be pulled back to the cave. Then you will know it is time to retrieve it."

"What do I do with it then?"

"I do not know. But you will know when the time is right.

Retrieve it and use it for good. It is not only important for our people, but for everyone alive."

"I will get it when the time is right, and figure out what to do with it."

Hia died soon after. It was an easy death and one she knew was coming in the way of her people. It was not easy for me. As soon as our youngest was of age I left that place and went after old enemies. Meanwhile the people ended up on the wrong side of a war and were decimated. Cowee Town was assaulted and burned to the ground, a fate shared by almost every other town. The few spared were depopulated by disease.

With all that happened within that brief span of time, including our son's death, Hia's death, the near eradication of the tribe, my pursuit of Governor Tryon, I forgot about Hia's trinket hidden in a cave of my distant past.

I also had thought about traveling through the links to go back and visit that happy time. But Kal's warning against travel to the past had convinced me that to do so was too risky. Even an inadvertent mistake during a trip could result in a nasty paradox that might not even be fixable. Caution kept me from ever trying it.

Though it had been well over two hundred years, lately I have been thinking about the cave and what might be there. Not strongly, but it was oddly frequent. I wondered if the time was approaching when I would travel to the cave and open it. I decided the urge was not strong enough, and to put it off until or unless one or more of our descendants mentioned a pull to the cave.

Just to be safe, a couple of years ago I asked Monk to rig up a sensor and mini camera that ran off solar power. I went back to the area to install it near the cave. I barely recognized the place as it had grown so much. Hundreds of acres below the ridgeline were now swarms of suburban homes. None were on the ridge yet, but building was still in progress and new roads were up on the shoulder of the ridge. The vertical drop of the upper ridge and bare rock should preclude building around the cave itself, but now I was worried about humans finding it and plundering the contents. It took some doing at night to avoid all the new people, but I made it to the hidden cave entrance and installed the camera.

Yesterday I had a strong urge to go and visit the area, almost to the point of a compulsion. Not to surveil the spot, but to go inside. Something is calling and soon I will have to act.

Later today I will have a conversation with Nan and ask if she or Jen or others have had any urges or dreams to go back to Brasstown. I am almost afraid of their answers. What type of ancient object could lie dormant in a cave for two hundred years, then call a group of people back to find it? I don't know of any relics with that power, and I fear that if it exists, maybe it should not. After Odin's gifts nearly unmade me, I know some things are not meant for humans to wield.

Chapter Twelve

Henry I

The man rode slowly across the dusty ground, all brown, moving toward a distant ridge that was a slightly different shade of brown. The only thing to break up the monochrome beige was a thin line of green ahead. Likely a small stream that passed for a river out here, watering a few trees and some scrub. The man passed the time talking to his horse as there was not another sentient creature for miles around.

"Hope this hunch pays off. I'm tired of chasing this one. Should have done had him months ago."

The horse plodded on without answering.

"Now don't be like that, Shen. I know you are sulking because you got the pack job this time while I got the human."

"Yeah, but it still sucks, Wol. I never thought we'd be traipsing all over this hellhole for this long." The voice came out a bit nasally as the horse did have a long face.

Anyone listening would not have understood them. The one that appeared human and the other that appeared horse were speaking an unknown proto-Siberian language never used by humans.

"That's how it goes Shen. On these assignments you know

from long experience that we must stay in character for the duration. Too dangerous otherwise."

"I know. But my hooves are sore after being in character this long and galloping all over this land. And those flies are all over me. I can't scratch my ass and it itches something fierce. Even if I could reach it the hooves wouldn't let me savor the scratch."

"Well, I ain't scratching it for you. Besides, it's got to be better than being a mammoth."

"Well, it is, mostly. It took me two weeks to get that smell out of my skin."

"Yeah, that was funny, in a disgusting way. Maybe you should have manifested as one that did not have scent glands the size of watermelons. Who knew a six-ton critter with meter long hair that couldn't wash itself would smell that bad? But I'm surprised you remember that far back. Why did you do that again?"

"We had to get out of that village quick, and I decided that instead of sneaking out as a weasel, I'd go big and scare them off us. Would serve them right for the poor treatment they gave us. Unfortunately, all that excitement got my creature's scent glands active and squirting."

"Don't remind me. I still get nauseous when I smell something like beaver scent. It's the only thing even close these days to the stench of mammoth spunk."

"Yeah, but turning into one did get my displeasure across to them, didn't it? Not sure if it the size that scared them or the stink."

"Maybe it was the size of the stink."

The horse and rider plodded on. Wol figured there were hundreds of variations of beige in this valley. And every version was boring.

"Are we in Wyoming, Montana, Idaho, or Colorado?" asked Shen the horse.

"Not sure, but it must be one of those. Last week we were in Wyoming, so I'll rule out Montana, but maybe throw in Utah."

"Now you're just messing with me. Wol never gets lost."

"That's right, I don't. Hey, you smell that water up ahead?"

"Nope, not yet."

"Guess you can lead a horse to water but you can't make him smart."

Shen the horse did not reply verbally but did raise his tail and reply with a fecal outburst.

Wol thought about the American West, something that was very new to him. The land not so much, although he could remember the massive glaciers that once covered the mountains, slowly evolving into a beautiful venue of vast sky and landscape. Well, except for this beige valley. But these European-derived humans were very new in his time frame. Some African-derived people were here too, but they hadn't exactly been volunteers. The humans were not so lovely. Most were miserable and wretched as there was not sufficient food and shelter for many of them. But he guessed it was better than the tenement cities to the east.

These people were also finding out that the flatter and warmer places that they wanted to settle only had two seasons – dust or mud. That made for an unattractive human populace. But he was not here to gauge the beauty or hygiene of the people. He and Shen were here to end the thing that was feeding on the poor stinking humans.

After stopping at the stream and refilling their stomachs, Wol filled the canteens and a small barrel for Shen. They were not far from a town, but it was always better to be safe and act like humans. Besides, Shen got to carry the extra weight. After a brief discussion they decided to spend the night camped near the creek bank and get to town tomorrow. It would be uncomfortable camping for humans, but it was preferable for Wol and Shen as they didn't have to behave like a human in a hotel, or a horse in a smelly stable. Again, not that Wol minded the hotel nearly as much as Shen minded the stable.

Not needing sleep very often, Wol built a fire, and they passed the time talking about the chase so far. It had been many miles and many months, but they finally felt they were getting close. To what, they weren't sure yet, but they intended to find out soon.

They were both aware of the sounds in the darkness.

"I believe we have visitors," Wol said. "You stay in horse mode until I determine who they are."

"Of course. But you know as well as I do that good people don't sneak up on a camp at night."

"True, but there is still some hope it's a mistake on their part."

"Go ahead with your giving of the benefit of the doubt. I'll be over here laughing when you have to turn into an armadillo to escape the bullets."

"Quiet, horse. Here they come."

Three men crept up quietly on the camp. At least they thought so. But both the man and the horse had heard them ride up and walk the past mile, then heard their heartbeats and gurgling stomachs for the past thousand meters. It was not going to be a fair contest.

Once the first gun clicked as the bandit cocked it, Wol disappeared into the brush behind him. He sped around and then behind the first gunman and swatted him on the head. He grabbed a leg and drug him toward the second gunman. Hearing the noise coming at him, the gunman yelled once then started shooting blindly toward Wol. That just pissed him off, so again he swiftly moved behind the shooter and swatted his head. Now he drug two humans toward the third.

"Jarvis, Slade, you still there?" the third bandit asked. "What the hell is going on?"

"What is going on, you dimwit, is that you gave up your location by yelling. Not that it would have done you much good to keep quiet. Now I'm dragging these two vermin toward you, and you should go ahead and drop your gun before you get hurt."

The third guy, determined to live up to his new nickname,

fired twice toward Wol's voice, then turned and ran toward the horse. He obviously had plans to grab it and ride out before Wol could get to him. Both bullets missed, but Wol noted the gun had a different sound than the one that had just shot at him.

Wol watched yon dimwit running toward the horse, slamming to a halt and screeching as the horse unbelievably stood up on its hind legs. The two front legs turned into human arms and the hooves turned into hands; the face turned mostly human. If that wasn't crazy enough, one arm whipped around and pulled a rifle from the saddle holster. Now that rifle was pointed at the dimwit. Too shocked to move, he stood there like a drunken idiot. Both of those things were true as he was an idiot and had been drinking heavily while sneaking up on the camp. The horse promptly dinged him between the eyes with the rifle butt, and the third bandit fell limp as he'd been poleaxed.

Wol continued walking into camp dragging his two prizes and hoping they did not have fleas. "Hey Shen, I thought you were going to stay in character."

"I was, but the moron was about to jump on me. Besides, did you ever see someone so surprised to meet a man-horse hybrid in these woods?"

"I suppose it was funny, and from the smell of him he's drunk, so no harm done. I'll tie them up and we'll dump them in town tomorrow."

"Yep, but they'll walk in. No free rides, I might catch something. They don't smell like they have bathed in months."

"I know, I'll put them downwind of us tonight. Hey, do you see this rifle he was carrying? Looks like something new." Wol worked the action to unload it, then reloaded it and sighted along the barrel. "Hmm, I think I like this and will keep it. It holds a lot of bullets so that I can scare a lot of humans."

"What kind is it?"

"According to this new language of English, if I have it right, this rifle is a Henry's Patent."

"Well, there you go, Wol, you are now the proud owner of a Henry."

The next morning before daylight, Wol woke up the men. Later he tied them together and they walked along in front of him as he rode the horse. On the way, Henry untied the men's horses and set them free. He had rather the men walk than get on a horse and try to escape.

"Hey dummies, what did you think to gain from attacking me last night?" Wol asked. He used English as that was the language now spoken in this land. Wol knew a hundred other languages, many of them dead, so English was not difficult to master.

"We been hearing about a bounty hunter coming this way," the formerly drunken bandit said. "We thought you was after us. Can't be too careful when there's one of you around. Most get trigger happy and drag in any dead body they shoot hoping they's a reward for it."

"I suppose I'm a bounty hunter of a sort. But I was not after you. But I suppose you'd still have shot me and stolen the horse."

"After what I seen last night, I know I wouldn't even want that horse. It's haunted. It ain't right."

Wol smiled and swatted the horse.

"Not sure a live horse can be haunted, but it was awful decent of you fellas coming out here though and giving me the chance of making some extra cash. And a nice rifle. What are you morons wanted for, anyhow?

"We tried robbing a train and a stagecoach. Didn't go so well for us but did get us on the posters. We are the Gulch Jumper gang. On account of the only reason we got away from the law after that stagecoach caper, is we jumped the gulch and the old sheriff and his deputies couldn't make it. Take care of my Henry rifle. It's the only good I brought back from the war."

"What war?" Wol asked.

All three of them turned their heads with looks of disbelief and shook their heads.

"What's yer name anyway? We'd like to know who got us."

"You can call me Henry."

Wol, now known as Henry, dropped off the miscreants at the sheriff's office at the next town. The sheriff did not have any wanted posters on them yet, but after a telegram was answered it did confirm the men were wanted but no reward was set yet. It was likely to be only a hundred dollars when a new round of posters were released in another month. Henry told the sheriff it was not worth waiting on and he could keep the men in jail, while he needed to move on after a bigger payday. He and horse headed north without staying overnight.

Two more days and there was another town ahead. But no sign of dust or smoke, nor any smells. They camped overnight at the ghost town of Bryan. Next day it was on to the town of Green River. It had a railroad and was a real town yet still small.

After tying horse to the post outside, Henry slid into the town saloon. Not much cooler in there than outside, and even worse it was lacking the breeze. Stuffy and sour, sweat and leather smells permeated the space. It was not conducive for polite discourse and gentlemanly behavior. The town thug leaned stinkingly on the bar, so Henry moved two steps further down and ordered two waters and a whiskey. He preferred the water, but he intended to add some whiskey to kill off the poor flavor of the old tepid water. The whiskey would at least slow the parasites swimming around, even though they were no threat to him. It seemed the right thing to do.

The thug smirked at his order. He was big, ugly, and projected an aura of menace. "You having a party with yourself or just too prissy to drink it straight?"

He ignored the man's jibe, pouring the whiskey into each filmy water glass.

"You heard me, priss. Answer up or you'll be leaving here the hard way."

He glanced up at the man with a smirk and then went back to

ignoring him. Henry decided to engage in the classic passive-aggressive behavior that usually elicited a response from town toughs. Amazing how they were all the same, all around the world, and in every era.

The thug had had enough and moved his hand to his grubby pistol, stashed in its moldy holster. Faster than anyone could follow, Henry took three steps and used his left hand to draw and slide the barrel of his pistol into the thug's right nostril, about an inch deep. He kept enough pressure that the man could not move his head.

"I'd suggest you not speak further. Or make any noise at all lest the vibration twitch my trigger finger, making that sound the very last you hear."

Then Henry used his right hand to take another drink of the whiskey-flavored water he had brought with him. The rest of the saloon had gone quiet. Most had probably not seen the town thug bested so easily or quickly. But Henry knew some town toughs, always stupid and mean, sometimes had allies and backup plans. He felt a smaller man take a position behind him. He had noticed when walking in earlier that this man wore his pistol lower than normal and there was no mold on his leather holster.

Without looking over his shoulder, Henry said "Walk away and live. Stay behind me and die."

The man on the end of Henry's pistol barrel slightly flinched his eyes. Probably worried his buddy's round might pass through and hit him, or that his tormentor's reflexes after being shot might relieve the thug of a necessary but seldom-used piece of his anatomy, his brain.

It was a moot point. Henry's right hand blurred to pull and fire a hidden pistol without taking his eyes off the thug. The bullet entered the second man's head dead-center between the eyes. The man's hand was on his gun, but he had not been able to pull it before his nervous system collapsed. Henry normally did not seek out violence, but he felt it was a good idea in this case. Best to have a reputation as the new bounty hunter not to be messed with.

Addressing the man in front of him, Henry slid his pistol barrel from the nose and wiped the moisture on the man's dirty shirt.

"Why don't you be of use and fetch the sheriff?" The thug literally ran from the bar.

Chapter Thirteen

Henry II

An older gentleman soon entered the bar wearing a star on his shirt. Whipcord thin with piercing eyes, he was the epitome of a sheriff in the Old West.

"I see Gentry's got himself a new look, mostly dead. Mister, would you mind walking with me over to my office?"

Henry nodded and followed the man out. He winked when he went past horse tied up outside.

"My man in the saloon tells me he's never seen anyone faster. Nor has he seen shooting that accurate without looking." The old sheriff was direct and concise, both of which Henry appreciated.

"I'm a bounty hunter working alone. Skills like that improve my longevity."

"I can see that. Still, seems uncanny. You staying here long?"

"Not planning on it." The sheriff tried to hide his pleased look. Henry pulled a folded wanted poster from his pocket and handed it to the sheriff. "Looking for this person."

"I see there is no reward on this poster. What's he done?"

"No reward because the official law has not caught up to him. He rides into town, stays a day or two, then slaughters a family. He's usually in their house a few days after the killings."

"I heard something like that a few weeks ago, a town back to the southeast."

"That was him."

"Why does he stay in the house after the killing?

"He's feeding on the family."

"What? Oh god, that's horrible!"

"Yep, that's why I'm after him. I won't quit until he's dead."

"How come he ain't been caught, or at least made the wanted posters?"

"He's been at it a while so he's good at covering his tracks. He comes into town and keeps a low profile while casing the town for a couple of days. Then he locates a family on the edge of town that is not likely to be disturbed for a week. Kills them and feeds a few days. He dumps the bodies in old mineshafts around, or the nearby river if it's big enough, or he fires the house. Takes their horses and wagon, or the train, and travels one to two weeks to the next town. He gets fifty or a hundred miles away before the family shows up as missing."

"That's terrible but makes some sense. Not that unusual for a family to up and leave, and nobody is gonna look too close at a burned body to notice if any parts are missing."

"Yep, and he changes his appearance. Might be bearded or clean-shaven, long or short hair, or bald. He might be dressed like a farmer, cowboy, or banker. Uses a different name in every town and never stays long. A constant drifter but well-dressed enough to not cause any concern. Never says anything but his name, whatever it is that day. Most unusual fellow but deadly beyond telling."

"That could be anyone showing up new in a lot of these towns. Between the mines, the cow herds, and the railroads there's new folks every week."

"That's why it's so hard catching him. At least until now. I've got a lead that he might be around or is coming through here on the way north."

"Well, I hope you catch him, and quick. If I see anything I can send a deputy for you."

"I'll be on the road north. Thanks sheriff."

Henry left and got on horse. The sheriff was not exactly unfriendly, but Henry knew the man wanted him gone from town. Probably before the dead man's friends got liquored up enough to seek retribution, and somebody else got killed.

"We been after this thing for months," said Shen, the horse. "Back in Siberia him getting away so long would make sense cause it's so wide open. But here, with all the people, in a small country, seems like we should have been done long ago."

"Only somebody like us from Siberia would think this place isn't wide open. But I know what you mean, we shoulda tied this up two months ago."

"You think it's shifting, or just smarter than us?"

"I think it's because it is something different. We've run down all sorts of wendigoes, vampires, and dozens of other things and put them down, right enough. But this one don't fit, or maybe don't feel like anything I've chased before."

"I'll agree on that. Don't seem to act like other vermin, and the few times we got close enough, it didn't smell like anything I know either. And that's saying something considering how old we are."

"Yep."

"You ever run across anything before like this that don't make sense, or fit into any category we've chased?"

"Just once before. A little over a century ago, back east in the mountains, toward the other coast. I was snooping around and ran across a Nunehi shifter, a real powerful one. She shown twice as bright as most of them, all gold-like."

"Yeah, they are real nice people. That must have been something to look at."

"This one was, too, although I never got close enough to meet up. I was careful not to show myself because she was mates with a fellow the likes of which I'd never seen before. He was all silvery. I could tell he was real powerful too like a Nunehi. But completely different."

"Was he a bad one? But I couldn't see a Nunehi living with that."

"Nope, at least not any worse than you or me. Their children were something, too. Definitely Nunehi and good folks, but they had something of their father in them too. Still do, as I stayed curious enough that I still go check on them ever couple of decades."

"What happened to the shifter and her odd man?"

"She passed on after a time like they normally do. According to stories, he got back on a boat and went back east to the white continent, where he came from."

"Huh, wonder if he passed on over there."

"Don't know. But the offspring are here, some in the Oklahoma Territory and some still back east. I got a feeling they are around for a reason, but I don't know what it is, at least not yet."

"You ever thought above going over to find him?"

"Nah, you know how they are over there. Too crowded both with humans and others like us. Doubt I'd be welcomed. But I expect if he survived, he'll eventually come back to visit family. Anyway, it's late, and I'm going to sleep an hour. You all comfy on all four hooves?"

"As always. But if I get to feeling colicky I'll do it your direction."

Henry and horse moved along the next morning. It was cool but the lack of clouds meant it was going to be a warm day soon enough.

"You remember how this place used to look?" Shen the horse asked.

"Well, you need to narrow that down," Henry answered. "The first time in this area all I saw was ice a thousand feet thick."

"Yeah, guess so. But a few hundred years ago. After the last big cull happened."

"It was nice, the land not much different than now. But more of our people were around, at least the ones left. Not all these white eastern people, their animals, and metal tracks."

"That is what I remember too. Is this new way better you think?"

"No idea, at least not yet. Time will tell how these new people work out. One day I got my doubts, the next it seems it might be alright. They tear up this land but can build a nice repeating rifle."

"I'm seeing the same. Beginning to think these people are dichotomous, and certainly disparate."

Henry brough the horse to a stop. "Shen, you are a Warden, and currently a horse. What the hell did you just say?"

"I'm practicing my new vocabulary. The stable boy was reading a book, something called a dictionary, sitting on the walkboards where I was tied up in town. I was reading over his shoulder. But I only got to see a couple of the D pages."

"Shen, did you set up this whole conversation just so you could use your fancy new words?"

"Kinda."

"You're an ass."

"Nope, I'm a horse."

They continued along the road. Horse tried to whistle but it came out as more a raspy whinny. Henry ignored him as it had been a few months too many together with his friend and colleague. But they had known each other for more than ten thousand years, so Henry was more forgiving of Shen's idiosyncrasies. Hmm, now he was going to have to work that word into conversation as payback.

In the middle of day, after a long trek through the beige heat, Henry saw a small dust cloud approaching down the road. Not surprisingly, the dust was beige too. They had passed two other wagons on the route, so it was not an unusual sight. A few minutes later Henry saw a one-horse carriage with one person approaching. A slight man, dusty but dressed nicely and wearing a bowler hat. Both he and Henry nodded as they passed without speaking. A second later Henry realized the man did not look right or smell right. And there was a unique smell coming from carriage. Shen the horse caught it and had already turned back to the carriage. The man on the carriage had also realized danger, and with inhuman speed leaped back over the carriage and with a second leap toward Henry. Or where Henry had been.

The fellow was surprised when what he thought was a horse was now a cave bear that he'd leapt onto. Henry could not see the surprise on his face because the man's whole head was inside the bear's mouth. Bear was shaking its head sharply from side to side trying to snap the thing's neck. Meanwhile the horse pulling the carriage galloped off once it sensed the bear.

Henry had jumped off the horse before the man had jumped from the carriage. Now he morphed into an American lion, more than a thousand pounds of ruthless carnivore. He went around the bear to slash the back and hamstrings of the thing while bear worked on the neck. Henry was amazed when neither his teeth nor claws could penetrate the skin. Bear seemed to also be unable to break the neck. Whatever the thing was, typical methods to kill it were not working.

The thing was fast, and seemingly impervious to injury, but was not particularly strong since it could escape the bear. Henry turned back to human form and went over the saddle lying on the ground since horse turning to bear had broken the cinch strap. He grabbed a knife, the rifle, and the coil of rope. He tried to stab the thing in the back but was not surprised when the blade didn't penetrate. Then he shot it, but the bullet ricocheted off, though it did leave an indention in the skin.

Well, if they could not kill it, they at least needed to incapacitate it. He picked up the coil of rope and stated looping around the thing, but thing was not cooperative. Henry had Shen-horse-bear clamp the thing's arms with his paws so Henry could bind its arms and legs. Once done, bear dropped thing and turned back to human. Thing was lying in the dirt struggling against the rope, with an unnaturally long tongue shooting out from small sharp teeth that lined the mouth.

"What the hell is this thing?" Shen asked. He was breathing hard, as cave bears were devastating animals, but did not have the stamina to fight more than a few minutes with its mouth full.

"I don't know. Never seen one before, and not sure I've heard of one quite like this."

"It's weirdly tough, but kinda weak. What are we going to do with it?"

"Not sure yet, but we gotta finish it off, it's too dangerous to leave alive."

"It is not going anywhere trussed up. Guess we can figure it out. Track down the carriage and throw it in the back. At least I can stay in human form."

"Nope."

"Why not?"

"I just shredded my clothes and got one change left. If you want to ride in the carriage as a human, you'll be naked."

"Damn. Guess it's back to horse."

Henry and Shen retrieved the carriage and threw the thing in back, along with the broken saddle. There was a smelly bag with raw liver and a human haunch in it that they tossed out. Henry drove the carriage while horse walked along. They chatted about what to do but came up with nothing that might work.

"I'm wondering about this thing. Almost has a little bit of vampire going on but has skin like a wendigoe. Could be a hybrid, but never heard about those things getting together."

"Me either, but makes some sense. Problem is that makes it even harder to come up with a solution. Can't get through the skin to take the head off and burning won't kill it if it is a hybrid. Guess we can drop it in a mine shaft and cave it in."

"But if it don't die somebody might dig it up someday. Say, I just thought of something. Remember that crazy place we went through a few weeks ago?

"Oh, that might just do it. Maybe ten days riding so we keep it tied."

"Yep, keep it tied and we stay out of towns on the way, so no questions."

Nearly two weeks later, the carriage arrived at one of the strangest places on the continent. Henry and Shen, back in human form with clothes, went around looking for the hottest, largest, and stinkingest hot spring pot they could find. After some scouting they found the worst one. They dumped the thing, now accompanied with two large boulders, into a massive hot spring in the Yellowstone basin. Although it was an unpleasant place, they camped a few days waiting to see if anything came up, but it never did. A few weeks later Henry saw Shen off from the San Francisco port, bound on a boat back to Russia.

Chapter Fourteen

Vanderbilt I

In 1903, I found George Vanderbilt in the forest on his immense property in Asheville. He had been out riding on a warm day and had stopped by himself in a grove of trees near a spring. I had watched him and a few riders start from the stables earlier, but the others had already turned back with the heat. I had come there to kill him. But very likely not, or so I hoped. I needed to talk him into helping make something greater than both of us.

Since I was in hunting mode, he never saw or heard me until I wanted him to, just a step behind him. I startled him badly. It did not help that I was wearing my deerskin leather hunters and moccasins. He probably thought bear/Indian/robber all at the same time.

"Hello George," I said.

He jumped back quickly. "Who the hell are you?" he asked.

"Well, that depends. I could be someone you don't know who ends up killing you randomly. I could be the person to help you achieve great success here with your assets before I fade away quickly and quietly. I suppose which is really your choice."

"You are mad. How did you get on the property? I can have you arrested."

"Not necessary. I am part of a group that acts as stewards of the mountains in this area, for the benefit of the greater good. We would like to partner with you, if possible, but we'd be a decidedly silent partner, forever. And you would get quite a bit of a certain kind of profit from the endeavor."

"Is that why you are dressed as an Indian? An escapee from the Asheville asylum, that's what you are."

"Now, George, I know this is difficult for you. But you need to save all this land that you can, or lose everything. I'm here today unofficially to warn you of what will happen if you don't provide protection for the forests and people here. We will talk more in a few days when I arrive as your guest. Then you will understand more after our trip, and we can plot a course of action."

"I don't know what you are playing at, but if you show up here again, I will have you arrested. Get off the property or I'll have the dogs after you," he shouted.

I smiled and then sprang away faster than he could follow. Might as well give him something to think about.

A few days later, I arrived at the newly finished Biltmore House. I came riding in a carriage, wearing a suit and carrying a small bag. The servant took my bag as we arrived at the front of the house, and I stepped from the carriage. Another servant opened the door and escorted me into the grand foyer.

"Your room, sir, is upstairs and on the left hallway," he said. "I will show you the way."

"Thank you." I followed him upstairs and eventually to the suite. This was a damn big house.

"After you refresh yourself, if you please there will be a reception downstairs by the library at four pm," he said, after placing my bag in the room.

I nodded as he left and closed the door.

I had plotted my strategy for some years and had intentionally met certain members of the Vanderbilt family, especially Edith. I was able to approach and make their acquaintance first in Europe and later in New York. As a man of means, and ostensibly Dutch,

112

with a perfect English accent and knowledge of America, it had not taken long to get invited to the house. I had arrived a week earlier than advertised so I could have my initial surprise meeting with George Vanderbilt. It wasn't the house I was interested in, but rather the more than ninety thousand acres of mountain land he controlled. That land could ensure the existence of my family or destroy most of their heritage by depriving them of the necessities they needed. I was going to get what I needed one way or another.

I washed up, changed clothes, and left my suit hanging on the door. It would be cleaned and pressed by the evening. Money could purchase enough servant labor to make life very easy for the 0.1%. Some things never change.

I walked downstairs, toward the back of the immense house, and then down the left side of the massive building. There was a loggia between the library proper and the magnificent open balcony on the rear of the house overlooking the French Broad River Valley and mountains beyond. Edith and several other ladies were standing and conversing while having light refreshments, while the servants, of course, attended to them. As I walked up, they all noticed, and Edith came up to me first.

"Sen, how wonderful you could visit us," she said. "Please have something to drink while I introduce you to my friends."

I air kissed her cheeks three times in the Dutch tradition.

I immediately had a mimosa placed in my hand. Edith introduced me around and told everyone I was a dear friend from Europe. That was all it took to give me full credibility in a room of strangers. We chatted nonsensically for the next half-hour about Europe and America. This was still the gilded age and before the nightmare of World War I, so we could all pretend the world was great. At least for those of us with money.

The ladies began filtering out to get dressed for the evening meal. A couple were quite attractive and one was even interesting, but I was not here to get distracted. Well, maybe just for an evening. I would likely never see them again after the week was finished.

I walked out to the balcony and Edith found me a moment later.

"I can't wait for you to meet George," she said. "He had business today or he would have been here already. I'm sure you will get along famously."

"I am sure of that as well, Edith," I responded. "I only have a few days, but I appreciate the chance to visit before returning to Europe. I hope George is available to discuss some minor business before I leave, otherwise I intend to enjoy the countryside while I am here."

"I am sure he will be available. He likes to ride and explore so I will also have him take you out to the far reaches of our little empire."

"Thank you, Edith. That sounds wonderful."

We walked back in the house and she went upstairs to change. I wandered into the library. Another servant offered me a brandy and cigar, both of which I declined. I was guessing there must be a servant in each room. I found a book, then sat and looked around the room and at the ceiling. I could not quite decide whether I liked the house or not. It was built to look like an old European mansion, but it was all new. It therefore lacked the charm of the old buildings, but also lacked the annoying drafts and smells and idiosyncrasies that made those old buildings so annoying to reside in daily.

I was quiet enough and the room large enough, so that when George came by the room, he did not see me. He was on his way upstairs. I would have welcomed a quiet chat, but he probably would have been upset enough to have a servant try to apprehend me. I don't think that even with all the servants he had, there would have been enough to accomplish that goal. I had an easy premonition that dinner would be interesting.

I went upstairs, then came back down well before the meal

was to begin. I was lucky in that Edith and one of her friends, the attractive and intelligent one I had been impressed with earlier, were in the foyer and strolling toward the back and middle portion of the house, where there was a closed porch. They saw me and stopped.

"Sen, come with Julia and I to see the thunderstorm over the valley before we dine," Edith said.

"I would love to accompany two such lovely ladies," I said, without laughing. I knew how to play the game.

We went to the porch and watched the lightning on the far mountains for a while and made more small talk. A servant came in and announced the meal was ready to be served. I took Edith's and Julia's arms in each of my own and escorted them to the dining room. As we entered, George was already seated at the head of a table that must have been thirty feet long. Some of Edith's other friends were in the room and seated while talking to George. He stood up as he saw the ladies, and then nearly choked as he recognized me.

"George, darling, here is my favorite European friend, Senecus Vogel, that I told you about. Sen has been a dear today and keeping Julia and I company. Please come meet him."

He walked toward us looking none too happy, but obviously controlling himself, as he knew the game was shifting. Until he knew more, he was not going to make a scene in front of his wife and her friends.

I unentangled my arms from the ladies and shook hands with George. "Great to meet you, George," I said with enthusiasm.

"Likewise, Senecus," he responded. Edith was frowning at him.

We all sat and began the first course of several. I was between Edith and Julia, and George was on the right side of Julia. Since there were only the four of us plus the other three of Edith's friends, there was no reason to follow the old seating style of George on one end of the long table and Edith on the other. Wine was flowing freely but had little effect on me. I spent most of the evening talking about Europe and making Julia laugh. I was still trying to decide if I should explore that opportunity for the next few evenings. George was pleasant but several times I noticed him looking at me, probably like a husband looks at the dangerous stray dog his wife has just let in the house.

As dinner ended, we all went back to the open balcony to watch the last of the storm. It had not crossed the valley, so there was still some lightning on the far mountains, which could only be seen during the flash. The ladies walked into the library for aperitifs, leaving George and I alone on the balcony.

"Nice place you have here, George," I said. "Edith really seems to like it."

"Yes, she does, and I like to please her," he said. "Which is why I have not called the sheriff yet."

"Obviously no need for that. I am just a gentleman from Europe visiting a dear friend in Asheville. Anything that would spoil that would just be crass. And unprovable." I had him by the short hairs and he knew it. And he did not like it.

"What do you really want?"

"Exactly what I told you previously. We should ride out to the west tomorrow, or the next day and I'll offer you a proposition which will make you happy. Then I'll leave and you will never see me again unless you and Edith want to visit me in Europe. I would be happy to host you both, along with your daughter, if you come to Holland."

"I have a meeting tomorrow, so our trip will have to be the day after. I warn you now that I will tolerate no threat to my family."

"I have made no threat to them, nor will I. In fact, I would protect them and everyone in this house if there was a threat of any kind. The stewards that I mentioned before can also protect you and your family in perpetuity should we come to an agreement this week."

"We will see," he said, then walked into the library.

Edith had been glancing out to where we were. She was still frowning. George was going to have to provide an explanation, or a believable lie. Meanwhile, I went over to Julia and restarted my understated charm offensive. It seemed to be working. Conversations continued, and Edith was no longer frowning. The other ladies were not so happy, however, as two of them were single and the room was now out of eligible men.

As the evening ended, I had no more conversations with George. Just as well, since Julia was monopolizing my time. As people began drifting upstairs, we all said our goodnights and would meet again tomorrow.

"Julia, may I escort you to your room?" I asked.

"Of course, you may," she answered. She seemed delighted to get me upstairs and away from the competition.

We strolled up the stairs and down the far corridor.

"Which room are you staying in?" she asked.

"I'm in the other corridor, with a pleasant view to the south and west," I answered. "Which is fortuitous because the moon is up tonight and outside my window."

"I have not been on that side. Do you mind if I take a peek?"

"Not at all, I think you will like it."

We went back to the other corridor and entered my room. She walked over to the window and was silhouetted in the moonlight.

"This is very nice," she said. "Quite the view."

"Yes, it is," I agreed.

Julia decided to stay a while and acquaint herself with a different room than hers. I was a perfect gentleman, at least most of the evening. She didn't seem to mind. As soon as the dawn sky brightened the window, she dressed and disappeared back to her room. Many years later that type of jaunt would be named the "walk of shame." But only if someone saw you.

I spent the bulk of the next day outside and walking the property. I had seen Julia briefly in passing in the house during a course of breakfasts. She smiled largely while the other ladies looked on without smiling. Taking a very long stroll seemed like a good idea.

The Biltmore property was incredible. Ninety thousand acres here, eight thousand acres there, an entire village built nearby, and thousands of additional acres designated for plantings, forestry, and recreation. I really needed to persuade George to preserve as much as possible. I thought it would be an easy sell, as he was already interested in sustainable forestry. And President Roosevelt was coming the following month, another influential person interested in conservation. Tomorrow would be a pivotal day for my people and this entire region for many years.

As I walked the massive spread, I thought about my ideas to preserve the countryside. There were irreplaceable and priceless coves, caves, and hollows in the mountains. Home to species not recorded yet. But timber companies were buying rights to timber all over the southern Appalachians and destroying habitat. Somehow it had to be stopped or at least slowed to provide some refuge for the species that were most threatened. Europe had already felt the effects of mass deforestation. Entire climates had been changed in the quest for materials for fuel, wooden ships, houses, and bridges. It would happen here next, then the locusts would move on to the next big forests in Canada or the Western US, anywhere to fell a tree and make a profit.

As I was thinking those negative thoughts, a shadow appeared in the woods beside me.

"Granddaughter, it is good to see you," I said to the beautiful young woman beside me, with her golden glowing skin that only I or her family could see.

"Greetings, and good to see you again so soon."

"Will the preparations be ready for tomorrow since we could not proceed today?"

"Yes, everything is ready, as are all of us. Do you think we will be successful?"

"We must be, as there is no choice anymore. Unless everyone

moves west and major changes are made, or stay here and completely lose the way of the people."

"I see it the same. I don't want to move west."

We did not say anything more but walked arm in arm for a long time. Sometimes the only positive thing about a long life was having a family that also lived a long time and could understand the anguish that could overtake an otherwise perfectly nice day. As the day wore on, she left me as quietly as she had arrived.

"I will see you tomorrow, my dear," I said.

"I will see you also, dear Fisher," she said, and she disappeared. Later, I saw a hawk flying across the valley. I didn't know if it was her, but it was a welcome sight either way.

I arrived back at the house in the late afternoon. I did not see anyone around but the servants, so I summoned a pitcher of lemonade and headed to the library. I had seen interesting books there earlier. George had already gathered over twenty thousand volumes, so I was sure to find something there of interest. I found a promising book and settled in for a while with it and my drink. I only had an hour or two before I went upstairs for a bath and to dress for dinner.

Everyone was back at dinner as per the previous evening. Julia seemed to be in a good mood, and the other ladies seemed to be in a slightly less good mood. If Edith noticed, she had the good manners to not speak of it. George was quieter than normal, but then he had been stuck in financial meetings most of the day. I don't think that was his strength. I know that I would rather chew my arm off than spend many days like that myself.

After dinner we wandered back to the loggia between the large balcony and the library. George and Edith were in the library and were having an earnest conversation. Julia had grabbed my arm and guided me to the balcony overlooking the valley. The other ladies stayed in the loggia with their drinks and were speaking in low tones. With my overactive hearing, I didn't have to wonder what they were talking about. It was mostly about

Julia and whatever would her husband think? Husband? I didn't have any idea she was married. Then I heard one of them say it did not matter, they had not been together in five years. Ah, there must be a back story. I decided it was best to not get involved. Plus, it was disorienting to make small talk with Julia while listening to the conversation of three other ladies.

George and Edith had finished their conversation, and he came out to talk to me. Julia went back inside to the library to chat with the rest of the ladies now attending Edith.

"So, we are going on a trip tomorrow?" he asked. "What time do we leave and where are we going?" His temper was not improved much. I was not sure whether that was due to me or his conversation with Edith. Probably both.

"We should leave early, around six in the morning. We can take three horses and will ride to the far western edge of your holdings. There is no reason we should not be back shortly after dark, so we will only need one days' worth of provisions."

"Three horses?" he asked. "Is Julia coming, and is that wise?"

"No, that would not be wise, and she isn't coming." Obviously, he was informed that Julia and I had been spending time together. "We will pick up a third person on the way." He did not look happy. I imagine he thought I was bringing a goon. "It is my granddaughter, Lilly, who lives in the area."

He now looked confused. "We are riding that far with a child?" I guess that by his math, my granddaughter would be a toddler, like his daughter.

"She is not as young as you might think," I said, as he looked skeptical. "It's a complicated story, but she has been riding for years and needs to come along."

"Everything about you is not what it seems, and is complicated, isn't it?"

"That is an accurate statement. But there is no risk or danger to you, nor subterfuge beyond a certain amount of necessary secrecy. And tomorrow you will know the secret and can then decide your response. And I will depart and leave you in peace."

That seemed to mollify him.

"I suppose we should retire then as we have an early start," he said. "I'll have the servants prepare our horses and necessary provisions. Goodnight and I will meet you at the stables in the morning."

I said goodnight as well, and he went into the library to tell the ladies goodnight and excuse himself. As he left, I saw Edith looking out at me questioningly, Julia looking at me with longing, and the other ladies trying to ignore me. I walked in to see them and also said my goodnights. I then walked back upstairs to my room, alone.

About two hours later, I heard a soft knock on the door. I would not be getting a full rest tonight after all.

Chapter Fifteen

Vanderbilt II

I was at the stables just after dawn the next morning. George was there while one of the stable hands was readying his favorite horse. Someone had already saddled two other horses. They were both fine animals, but older.

"I had two of the gentler horses prepared for you and your granddaughter," George said.

"Thanks, I am sure Lilly will appreciate your thoughtfulness." I was thinking she could ride us both into the ground. And that George, on his horse, probably thought he could outride and escape us if necessary.

We set out to the west with the sun rising behind us. Within a short time, we came to the French Broad River and crossed over, continuing across the wide valley on a dirt road. I had Lilly's horse tethered to mine. The fields turned into level woods, then foothills, and after that we were in the mountains and on steeper trials working towards Mount Pisgah. The trail was narrow, so I was behind George. I had a quick flash of movement, and when I looked back, Lilly was astride the rear horse. It flinched, but she quickly said something low in its ear and stroked its neck, and it was perfectly calm. We smiled at each other and quietly continued.

We rode another twenty minutes before George said, "I suppose your granddaughter is not joining us today."

"Oh, she joined us a while back, but did not want to disturb our ride," I said.

George made a sound, then turned his head back toward me. What he saw behind me was a beautiful woman on the third horse, wearing a green dress as nice as any as would be worn by the ladies at Biltmore. He was startled but regained his composure quickly.

"Lilly, this is Mr. George Vanderbilt," I said. "George, this is my granddaughter, Lilly Ward."

"Pleased to meet you, sir, and thank you for the pleasant ride today," Lilly said.

"My pleasure," he said. We continued on. George was getting better at playing the game. Then again, between his family and all the business dealings, he must have had practice keeping his emotions level.

We stopped along a brisk small creek for lunch. I told George we still had about an hour's ride to go. We finished our small meal and mounted up. And it was up, as the trail became very steep. After half an hour we topped a ridge and descended slightly into a high valley. The trail was gone, and we were in a small meadow with a bog on one side, while tall trees surrounded the opening. I stopped, as did Lilly. George noticed and wheeled his horse around to trot back to us.

"George, this is where the secrets begin," I said. "As we leave the edge of your holdings, I ask that you consent to be blindfolded for the next few minutes until we reach the final destination. Lilly will take the lead, and I'll be behind you to keep your horse docile. Of course, you can pull the blindfold off if your horse is unruly."

He did not look happy but allowed Lilly to put a black cloth across his eyes and tie it at the back of his head. I wasn't sure it would even keep him from seeing where we were going, but I figured Lilly would ride around in circles for a few minutes, so maybe that would work in combination with the blindfold.

We rode across the meadow and skirted the bog, then Lilly did a figure eight, then a half-circle before we left the meadow. We went into the trees and then descended slightly after ten minutes of riding. There was a thin waterfall ahead, and it fell about thirty feet into a depression, which was in reality a sink, on its way to being a sinkhole, with a diameter of twenty feet. The water pooled up there under the waterfall but there was no exit, it just disappeared into the earth. We stopped, and I moved up to George and grabbed the reins of his horse. Lilly pulled her horse to his other side and removed his blindfold.

"We are here," she said.

We all dismounted and tied off the horses. Lilly opened a small bag she had brought and removed three torches and matches.

"This is a nice hollow," George said. He saw the torches and added, "Ah, a cave, makes sense since the water disappears. Must be a bit of limestone in the area."

Everything I had heard about George indicated he was intelligent, very well read, and about as educated as any self-taught person in America. Being around him in person these few days proved that out.

We followed Lilly over to one side of the waterfall. There was a vertical slab of rock, approximately two feet wide and three feet tall. She bent down to grab it but George said, "Allow me please, Miss Ward."

She moved out of the way and George grabbed it but could barely move it, despite his exertions. Lilly smiled at him and said, "Thank you, sir, for your gallantry. But I am used to moving this stone so I will take care of it."

George looked dubious, but got out of the way. Lilly picked it up and set it to the side. George looked impressed.

"Grandfather, as you come last, please replace the stone so no one can find us by accident," Lilly said.

"Not a problem," I said.

Lilly leaned down and stepped in the cave entrance, then lit the three torches and handed two to George. She moved further back, and then George crouched and stepped in as well. I did the same, then turned around and grabbed the stone and set it back in place. George handed me the other torch, and we worked our way forward. After ten feet, the cave opened above us and we could stand normally.

"Once we get further in, there will be miner's lanterns, so we can snuff the torches and use them on the way out," Lilly said. We walked on another hundred feet or so as the cave opened to the sides. There was a wooden table set with lanterns, and also piled with a few dozen used torches. I knew what that meant but wasn't sure if George did: the rest of the clan was already here.

We lit the lanterns and had an easy walk as the floor was fairly smooth as it descended. There were images painted, mudded, and carved into the walls. George was entranced and kept slowing to look at the more elaborate art.

"This is amazing. Any idea how old this is?" George asked.

"A lot of this was long before the Cherokee came to these lands," I said. "Based on several observations, plus some of the cave art found in Europe, I would bet this is several thousand years old at least."

"Outstanding. I don't think anyone in America even knows about this. This is a whole field of study waiting to happen."

"A very few people know about this, and you are about to meet them," I said. I was trying to be mysterious, but I don't think he was really listening to me.

The cave opened up even further into a room the size of George's library. Thirty people were there, sitting in a circle on the floor. Some were dressed similar to us, others more like farmers or hunters. Some were obviously Native American, others more Caucasian. The Cherokee people were normally tolerant of who could join. That had worked for me in the past. George seemed surprised at the group.

"George, these people are my distant family, and many are Lilly's immediate family," I said. "Everyone, this is George Vanderbilt."

A chorus of voices said 'hello' and 'nice to meet you' from the circle.

"Also, George, these people represent the stewards of this land, roughly from Waynesville, North Carolina, to quite a distance over into Tennessee," I said. "There are more of them, but here today are the folks that were the closest to our meeting site."

"What is the purpose of the meeting?" asked George, getting right to business.

"Hopefully to convince you to keep and preserve the land you own, without clear cutting or mining most of it, in order to maintain the ways of mountain life for the benefit of these people and humans in general," Lilly said. Murmurs and nods of agreement came from the circle.

"We would hope you can convince others to do the same," I added.

"Is that all?" George asked. "You aren't asking me to give the land back, nor wanting any kind of payment, you just want me to preserve it?"

We all said yes. He thought for a second, and then asked, "But since it is my land, I will ask as a devil's advocate: what would happen if I did clear cut and mine these lands?"

"There would be an irreparable loss of habitat and life and these people would have to move west, most likely. Of course, people are not always what they seem, are they, George? Some plants, fungi, and animals would be lost that cannot be replaced. Some of the flora and fauna have already been shown to have strong medicinal purposes, so losing them could be catastrophic to future medicines. The idea is to preserve the land and all the ecosystems for that reason. The caves full of art should be protected and studied as well. And these people here would be the stewards, including for you and your family."

"I'm not sure how that applies exactly, or should mean much to me, other than just knowing that they are grateful," George said.

"But these are not just people, George." In an instant, the people in the circle vanished and were replaced with animals instead. Mostly birds, plus a wolf, a mountain lion, and two black bears.

Now George was astonished. He quickly turned toward Lilly and me, but it was just me and a hawk.

"What the hell?"

"It's OK, George, it surprised the hell out of me, too, the first time I saw this."

"Is this real?"

"Yep."

"What do you turn into?"

"Absolutely nothing. Other than an ass occasionally. Although my story is even stranger than theirs. This is not the time or place for that. Do you now see how special this land is?"

"Yes, I suppose I do."

"OK, people, you can transform back."

George was quite perplexed when a completely nude Lilly reappeared beside us. After a second of looking at her, which I understood for him was difficult not to do, he spun around quickly to avert his eyes. Then he was looking at thirty naked people.

"Oh, my," was all he said.

Everyone dressed quickly.

"George, I would like to introduce you to these people and hear their stories before we go. I would also like you to have some time to see some of the unique art in this room. But we need to leave in an hour or two to get back at a reasonable time tonight.

You can talk with them further if you would like as most live in the area."

"Yes, I would like to talk to them now and again later in more detail. We can meet at the house, in town, or in the woods, wherever they will be comfortable."

We mingled like it was a cocktail party, rather than a cave full of shapeshifters. We could be social when necessary. After an hour and a half, it was time to leave. George had briefly met everyone and had more time to look at some bird and spider glyphs, plus some blown hand paint in the cave. As the three of us gathered to walk out of the cave, I noticed George blush when he looked at Lilly. She noticed, too, and just smiled at him. We took the miner's lamps and walked back halfway through the cave, traded them for the torches, and after lighting them made it back to the entrance. Lilly moved the slab. We all went out, and I put the slab back. The others would be out shortly, but there was no reason to be slack on discipline. This cave was one of many, but discovery by outsiders would probably lead to its destruction.

We untied our horses, mounted up, and left. We did not put a blindfold on George and I don't think he even noticed, as he was lost in thought.

When we got back to the meadow, he said, "I will do it. I was going to look into long-term preservation anyway, but it now seems even more important."

"Thanks George. I hope you or others can convince other large landowners to do the same. I know it may be impossible, but the amount of land that needs to be preserved is probably a million acres."

He looked shocked. "All my holdings are only ten percent of that. How would you even attempt to get the rest?"

"I don't know yet, but we intend to begin discussions with a wide range of people. Hopefully, you can get us contacts as well. I know Teddy Roosevelt is visiting here next month and it would be good to get federal support, although I know they take years to move on these issues. Large pieces of private preserves surrounding a national park, like Yellowstone, could accomplish much of that goal. What the Cherokee nation has accomplished with the Qualla purchases has been remarkable, but fifty thousand acres is not enough. Even if all the land were for sale, I don't think all of us combined could buy the million acres, so we need a novel approach."

He nodded and said, "That sounds reasonable, even though it is unlikely the timber owners will comply, at least until after the land is clear cut."

"Some cutting could be tolerated if it gains us the larger goal," I said. "But some portions cannot be cut or mined at all. It is more about management than total protection. Even if all the land was completely protected, a storm, landslide, or forest fire could still destroy some areas."

"That is logical. I also have talks scheduled with a German forester soon that may be helpful. I think I can work out a plan to accomplish the goal, at least on my property, and possibly sell the idea of preservation to others in the area. President Roosevelt seems amenable to preservation but he will have to be cultivated."

"It is a start."

"What is your story?" he asked me as we began descending the ridge and back toward the house.

Lilly laughed and said, "You should not have asked him. His story makes us look common in comparison. But we have a few hours left on this ride."

He looked interested.

"OK, George, you probably won't believe any of this. Now that you have met me and one of my granddaughters, go have another look at a particular volume I saw in your library."

I gave him the name of the book and the page number. What I didn't tell him was that it was an illustration by one of Bartram's peers, and it depicted Hia and myself in the late 1700s. Lilly looked very much like Hia so the resemblance would be unmistakable. That should give George either more reason to believe me, or think he might be going crazy. I began my long tale of multiple lives over multiple centuries. It passed the time on the way home.

The George Vanderbilt project ended up protecting a large piece of the Appalachians. The rest of the plan's success was more variable. As I look back over the last hundred years, I can definitely say it was a success; I can also say it was mostly a failure. We never got close to a million acres total. Certainly not any contiguous acreage that was even a portion of that size. But we got George's acreage, which became the basis for Pisgah National Forest after he died unexpectedly young; we got the Nantahala National Forest; we got Joyce Kilmer Forest, eventually, although much later; and through Teddy Roosevelt and other conservationists, we got the Smoky Mountain National Park. Those tracts, plus the Qualla area, made a difference. Part of the failure in the project was not getting some areas in time before they were clear cut or mined, and never getting the contiguous acreage needed to preserve the area completely. But it was enough to save some things.

What I never expected from that effort is how it would affect my family and I, and how it would lead us toward saving humanity. Even more unexpectedly, that would catapult me into an entirely new world of time travel and teleportation. My message from that project was that doing good things resulted in unexpected returns. It was the turning point in my post-Tryon days, as I finally reverted to a more positive life.

Chapter Sixteen

Danu I

I no longer know what I am. I remember most of what I was but acknowledge there could be large gaps of which I am not aware. Perhaps I have earned the right to forgetfulness after trying to remain in physical form for more than 60 million years. I know my memory has problems. I am sure that parts are missing, and sometimes feel that some things I think happened did not. Perhaps I went insane for ten million years, recovered, and did not even know it. The following account includes the portions I remember and think to be true.

My people originally came from Mars. The fables tell of us fleeing the failing planet surface for another world with water. The nearest planet had plenty, but it was not exactly welcoming. But we adapted and survived. Those same fables say that we invented spaceflight and moved ourselves. As a scientist and logician, I find that unlikely. My belief is that we were transported as it seems unlikely that we developed space travel and then lost that ability. More probable is that the entity in the Mars moon provided the means. The same entity that went insane and tried to kill us much later.

Our new planetary home often tried to kill us, but we managed the threats or fled from them. We progressed in part due to our unique environmental and physical adaptations. That manifested into advanced mathematics. We had many tentacles, multi-lobed brains, multiple sexes that changed as we grew, and everything we knew in our environment was spherical or spiral. From that, our mathematics developed accordingly, resulting in astounding leaps in knowledge. Problem solving was based on spheres and spirals rather than straight lines and right-angles from the beginning of our intelligence. That propelled our science beyond most civilizations in this sector of the galaxy.

But to realize the maximum benefit we had to change ourselves. As a people we decided to become hybrid lifeforms adapted to land. In a few generations we re-engineered our bodies through quantum genetics. At the time, the land was also dangerous for us, so we built a floating city. Once in our new form and dealing with gravity, more of a problem out of the water, we quickly we solved the problem and used gravity to propel vehicles and assist in building. Of course, moving into space travel was the next step.

Propulsion based on gravity or antigravity was simple and produced light ships since so little space or weight was dedicated to power systems. The right math and right materials made it easy. The rare elements we needed were harvested from the bottom of the ocean or filtered form the sea itself. I have watched the inept space attempts by the humans recently. Their technology based on oversized bullets is so inefficient and ill conceived. Humans will eventually give up such nonsense. Gravity systems are a magnitude more efficient with much less chance of malfunction. We were proud of the accomplishments that advanced math and willingness to change ourselves brought to us. But going back to space was both our salvation and undoing.

Unknown to us, we had fulfilled the necessary requirements for us to ascend. Although it sounds like more than it really is. Ascension is the ability to shed physical bodies, maintain full consciousness, and travel without the encumbrances associated with matter. But it also means interacting with other entities in the galaxy, with new requirements and restrictions on such "citizenship" in the galactic civilization. As we ventured outside the solar system, we came to the notice of the galactic powers. That is how we came to our next major change as a people, as we could choose to ascend and leave our physical forms behind.

As we left our planet, we also gained the notice and ire of the being or intelligence living on Deimos, Mar's smaller moon. It was a myth to us, but it was there and now insane. The Deimos fiend captured one of our ships and killed the occupants. It announced via the communications device that it would kill all of us. Since the location of our city was in the ship's navigation, we knew it would come for us.

We secretly set up a base on Earth's moon and ferried up whatever we thought we may need to continue our civilization. Which was kind of pointless as we had begun the ascension process and really did not need those things other than for reminiscing. Or as a legacy to the next sentient species to grow on Earth.

My people were lucky to have advanced so far. Far enough to detect an ancient insane menace that wanted to wipe us out. Far enough that we could ascend and secretly escape Earth and move into the galaxy. But we were learning of the terrifying entities in the galaxy beyond the insane god living in a Mars moon.

Were my people seeded on Mars? Why were we given the chance to move to Earth? Why did we not move underground on Mars to follow the water? We likely could have thrived there. Why was a guardian inhabiting our solar system, likely helping us relocate? Why was it now ready to smash sentient life on the verge of ascending? Those unanswered questions goaded me to set up secret plans to interfere and influence the new Earth, giving subsequent species the best chance of success. A new species would need to be much tougher than we had been to survive the new world, plus the extra-planetary threats. I was in the minority among my people, but I knew this asteroid strike would not be the last strike against the planet that had been our home.

Always planners, my people had already begun efforts to create new species for reseeding Earth after our departure. I was in charge of that project until the day I left my people behind. My efforts were preliminary and based on the trial and error of our species. I settled on a mid-sized land-dwelling biped, with dual sexes. Many of the details would wait until I saw the environment would be after the asteroid strike. I drafted out twenty different types of lifeforms to cover most anticipated climates.

The project made me rethink not only my role, but the underlying fabric of my people. Blunt recognition told me that our attempts at reseeding would likely fail as my people were too timid and conservative to develop a successful new life form. I was not sure my people would be chosen to return and reseed the planet, but it seemed a logical conclusion. But I knew my people were conservative and would adhere to the rules given to them by others in the galaxy. Rules that would likely condemn the next race to a catastrophic and untimely end, whether by a rogue menace or by an extraterrestrial invasion.

That is why I decided to rebel against my people, return to earth and secretly prepare and accelerate the next seeded race to face those extraordinary threats. I began my radical plan to offset my people's strategy. I had no idea how incredibly long the plan would take.

After ascension, I engineered and then hid the physical form I would take when back on Earth. It was partially based on our old forms when we were water dwellers. It was easy for ascended forms to track other ascended, but more difficult to track physical bodies, so I would revert to a physical form. The spaceship I had secreted away had been filled with tanks of water and the additional physical water forms I had engineered. Once the asteroid hit, but before we evacuated the moon for other worlds in the galaxy, I would flee to Earth.

I had bioengineered two tentai of myself. This was my old number system referring to the number of our tentacles; one tentai which was equal to eleven in human numbers. My brain sometimes thought in terms of my old water body form, which was most unlike our ascended essence, which was a nebulous existence. I rather enjoyed creating the new but retroactive physical form that allowed me to revel in the waters.

I created these twenty-two life forms based on more successful life forms that had survived in the Earth's waters in my species time but modernized them somewhat, and added armor and the ability to liven land for short periods. It was a risk to divide myself, or rather my consciousness into that many different life forms, but I knew many would not survive the coming millennia. I needed one to survive and be successful to fortify whatever species colonized the reseeded planet.

After the asteroid hit I flew the spaceship away from the moon to an Earth orbit. I could see all the continents as I circled the planet. Compared to today, six of the continents then were mostly formed and recognizable for their modern descendants, although Africa and South America contained large ocean inlets. The exception was Europe, which at that time was a series of islands and shallow seas, and no Mediterranean Sea. It looked little like it does now, but it was a good environment for water creatures. I also saw southern North America where our city had been; now it was a glowing crater filling with water and blowing out massive gusts of steam. I descended to a group of islands in the area of pre-Europe.

After landing I entered my one life form to ensure I could adapt to the body. It worked and now I felt safe from detection. The trickiest part of my entire project so far was then separating my ascended essence into multiple but equal portions of consciousness and inhabiting all the new forms. To do so I returned to my ascended state, then began dividing myself and entering the additional water forms. It was successful but incredibly disorienting. After two days I, or rather we, left the ship. It was instructed to burrow into the mud and remain hidden until or if I needed it. Literally indestructible and with an infinite power source fueled by the planet's gravity, it should survive anything. We entered the waters and dispersed into the seas and oceans anywhere that was habitable and began the wait. All of the forms kept in contact with each other via an embedded quantum entanglement system. I had lost the ability for telepathy after leaving the ascended state.

The carnage and damage to Earth was more extensive than predicted. I, or rather my multiple water forms, waited for higher life forms to develop. And waited for hundreds of centuries, then thousands. Nothing. I thought the reseeding would soon come, but it did not. I had miscalculated. My people had correctly estimated the damage from the asteroid and the likely time the Earth needed to recover before reseeding began. What we had not anticipated, but should have, were the Deccan traps. The asteroid impact caused immense volcanic activity at the antipode, or other side of the planet, upon impact. Immense lava flows spewed across the Indian subcontinent long enough to poison the planet. Several magnitudes of excessive damage were caused by the flows, and the Earth's biosystems cascaded into disaster.

My forms were engineered to be nearly immortal and able to survive most natural disasters. But I had not imagined such a scale of catastrophe. Some of my forms were caught in massive natural disasters. It was not possible to survive a surprise volcanic explosion. So much time went by that a few forms went insane and beached themselves to die. Eventually only a few of my forms were left. Continents continued to change, but the main difference for me was the slow coalition of islands and seabed that became Europe. Then, in fits and starts, the Mediterranean formed. Then it nearly dried out but refilled again five million years ago. By that time I was so thinly distributed that some major events completely escaped my notice. I also realized much later that fragments of memory must be missing. Therefore, what I relate is only what I can piece together from the more than 60,000 millennia that I waited to recombine into a single sentient being.

Also, something unexpected happened. It aways does when we engineer life. As my forms died, my very essence dissolved into the waters. What I had not expected was that the DNA strands entered micelles that formed in the water, then those began replicating. And replicating. For millions of years. The endless waters began filling with my essence and I could do nothing about it. My physical DNA, or at least strands of it, was out there in quantity. Yet because I had previously ascended into a different form altogether, but then reverted to physical form, my ascended essence was imbued into my DNA. Again, something unexpected and unintended. That ensured my survival at a basic level, but unfortunately with no way to proceed with my plan unless at least one of my major engineered forms survived to pull me together. So how long did I need to survive? Six hundred thousand centuries, it turned out.

Chapter Seventeen

Danu II

For many millennia after I had given up all hope for the planet's reseeding, I felt the arrival of new beings. But I realized they were familiar, and that my people had returned. Ironic that my people were the ones sent back, but I had predicted they would be the likely group chosen for the task. It was to my advantage as I knew them well enough to operate within their systems but never draw their attention. They would never suspect I had survived millions of years in a physical form on the planet.

They began setting up locations for reseeding. The nearest one was in Europe along a river. Three others were set up and my remaining forms went to watch the experiments develop. Several hundred thousand more years went by as forms were tested and perfected. For me the time seemed to pass quickly. I waited, knowing that the selection of the final form to seed the planet would take time.

I knew my people were conservative and would try many forms to reseed the planet. These first species would be designed to be very hardy in order to conquer the planet. I also knew they would be supplanted by other forms as the program progressed. What surprised me was that the majority of new forms were land-based and close to my original designs. Instead of making new life in their adopted land form images, they had learned from their mistakes and were concentrating on forms that had a higher chance of succeeding on this "new" planet.

Some of those initial models of precursor species went rogue. Unfortunately, some of them had been created with great powers compared to the simple life forms on the planet. My former people had difficulty tracking and eliminating them. Although they would occasionally catch one, there were always more. There were too few of me to attempt to reign them in. I knew they would cause problems, but it would have to wait until much later.

I had to be careful not to draw attention from the precursor models as they were too close to my colleagues and would betray my presence if I approached. The rogue ones were dangerous to approach since they were powerful enough to kill my physical form.

During the time of waiting for the successful dominant form to emerge from testing, I decided to create backup plans. First, I tried to inject dolphins with my serum, plasma, and DNA as I thought they were most likely to evolve and move to land. I knew that process would take too much time compared to influencing mammals already on land, but I needed to start experiments. Unfortunately, the dolphins died at the initial levels I used. My tissues caused strong allergic reactions and could not be tolerated. Yet smaller doses of my form, when ingested raw by the dolphins, did make some impact on their microbiome and improved their intelligence. But it was going to take even longer than I had previously thought.

I considered whales but knew instinctively they would never become land dwellers in time. Lastly, I tried the largest species of octopus. It was a complete failure as they were able to completely reject my tissues. No reaction, just rejection. It was a mystery, but I spent no time considering the ramifications.

Thousands more years passed. Finally, there seemed to be a contingent of seeded survivors that began to populate the land, albeit slowly. My former colleagues also began pulling back from their oversight to let evolution and selection play out with little interference as the new dominant species, called humans, developed. My former people were careful not to reveal themselves. The remaining guardian species, most of whom appeared human, became the primary caretakers of the humans during this time.

I watched the resourceful but primitive bipeds, waiting for opportunities to contact them. I needed to act soon to fortify the new species for the difficulties they were likely to face. My few surviving forms began attempts to interact with these new humans. The most significant problem from the start was the incompatibility of my DNA with theirs. Since my species were originally animals similar to large waterborne cephalopods, with reengineered DNA to adapt to land, I expected difficulties. But it was worse than difficult.

Whether due to the alien nature of my DNA or the essence imbued within it, it became clear it was incompatible with human DNA. Yet, I knew from the dolphin work that there were other ways to infiltrate foreign DNA into new forms without killing the test subjects. But those methods were much more subtle and could take years, and multiple generations of subjects. I had time to proceed with caution, yet I felt I needed to act soon.

Two of my forms, of the four remaining, approached multiple settlements near water sources. The forms were always rejected and chased off, even if bringing gifts of food. After that I was able to form short and very sharp silicate "needles" on the end of some of my tentacles. I could even shoot them short distances. Each needle had tiny drops of my serum or plasma that contained DNA and proteins. I injected that into the bipeds I found in the shallow coastal waters or in rivers. It never worked and those humans died terrible deaths and drowned. In those places I ended up in oral traditions as a sea monster.

I tried further experiments and approaches. One of my water forms tried to interact with humans by bringing gold, but success was limited. Physical contact was too much for them, and several died after contact with my form through allergic reactions. I called up my ship as it had survived and contained a basic lab. I was able to modify some parts of my DNA enough that it might not kill humans so quickly, and added a basic engineered virus. I hoped that would give the humans a better chance of survival as it greatly improved their health and longevity. But I needed other delivery methods and decided to sacrifice two of my forms.

Each approached human settlements and acted aggressively. The humans were enraged and killed those forms. It was what I wanted, because if they ate my remains, I could populate their microbiomes. But they did something unexpected and cooked my flesh before eating. Most of the proteins and DNA were denatured and useless for colonization. Yet a small amount did pass through, and in combination with the virus, gave my essence a small foothold with this group of humans. It just was not enough to give the maximum effect. There was enough that they gained some intelligence, but most of the effect was giving them long and healthy lives compared to the other humans on the planet.

One of my last two forms stayed nearby, occasionally bringing gifts of gold and jewels. Within a generation I was able to communicate enough with them to lead them to a Maker facility somewhat near their settlement. I could access it as my DNA was able to pass the first level of security and operate a key left for emergencies. The humans were able to retrieve a few items I guided them to, and for which I was able to instruct them to use. Almost all the other items in the facility were too advanced for them to use, or worse, to mistakenly misuse.

Years later a violent volcanic eruption began near them and killed my form. My last form went to them, and I was able to ferry them in my ship to a new and more geologically stable place, a large verdant island. I left them there and traveled widely in my ship looking for other groups, hoping I could find and a more advanced people. But none of them were much past the early stages of agriculture and science.

I could engineer and deliver more of my modified DNA, but since I was the last form, I was not ready to die with only a slight chance of my flesh causing a colonization of another group of humans. I tried other indirect methods, such as putting small amounts of my flesh in other fish and leaving it for the humans, but they either cooked or smoked and dried the fish, severely limiting any effect. More direct efforts of introducing my tissues or fluids into live humans always resulted in their deaths, usually in minutes or hours. My proteins were too allergic for humans to tolerate in undiluted form. The lab on my ship was inadequate to find a solution, or produce new forms of me to sacrifice. I found that my flesh with DNA, virus, and essence, had to be consumed, and freshly, to colonize the microbiome.

During this period, I was aware of another presence occasionally visiting the planet. Engineered viruses were released that produced negative effects on the human population. I did not have the ability to combat the contagion with my basic lab. The Guardians at first were unaware of it since they were immune, and then it was too late as the viruses spread. The viruses were complex but inelegant, so I knew my people were not involved. But I knew there were outside entities interfering and causing harm, and I would deal with them when I could.

My last form, the only me left, grew weak. I was not sure why, but I knew my time was limited. I his my ship again. Unexpectedly, while resting in a river, a human fell on me. Sword strokes severed my spine and damaged my gills. Sensing this was my last chance, I managed to push tissue and fluids into the human. The human had just been touched by something powerful and was even now assimilating an unusual but powerful virus. Then my body ceased to function, and I sank to the bottom. My time was over. All that was left were the uncountable particles of me in the waters of the planet and what was in the human.

My experience of time and sensory input ceased. Things happened but I was barely aware of it and had no way to act. This was death by dispersal. Amazingly, some tiny form of me began to grow again. I was inside a human. Maybe the one that killed me? Somehow, I survived, as did the human. After time I realized he was being treated and healed intermittently. I slowly grew in consciousness at the same time I was learning what it was like to be human. I managed to heal the human, called Senecus, of most of the worst effects of the old engineered virus over time.

Another unexpected turn happened. The human that I knew as Senecus gave a part of my essence to another human, a female. Not only did she accept the essence, it healed her, including from the old engineered virus. I had enough sentience to guide the process along and prevent complications. And another of me came into existence, in a sense. Inhabiting a female human form was a revelation as well. I could communicate with Jo, but very carefully through her subconscious so as not to influence her or take over any of her mind. Doing so would be to commit unimaginable wrong, making me no more than a harmful parasite.

Soon after, the human became pregnant. In a process that I cannot explain that event shocked my entity into full sentience. Now I had to tread even more carefully to not influence this new and precious life. Her pregnancy was unexpected but obviously a result of my essence affecting her body. Yet somehow the miracle of new life also restarted my life. I became me again. The tiny particles of what were once me coalesced into an amorphous version of my ascended body, but now I was bipedal and in a female form patterned roughly from Jo. I was aware of and able to sense input from the environment, first through Jo, then through my own senses.

I stayed inside Jo, but I knew I needed to leave before the baby gained any strong sense of self as I knew I better than to imprint on her. Surprisingly there was still a connection formed. It was then I discovered something profound. The baby was not truly

146

human. It, or she, was human plus, a prototype or hybrid of human on the cusp of ascension. Was it an effect of my clearing Jo of the engineered virus? Or my nearby essence influencing the process? Regardless, she was something new and a leap of evolution in human development.

My consciousness left Jo, while my basic essence remained with her, and I filtered into the water nearby. It was there that I fully realized just how strange everything had become. Uncounted particles of my being permeated the waters of the planet. Not sentient or conscious at all, but they all recognized me, and I could pull them to my will with great effort. It would take some time to determine how to use that ability. I knew it was too diffuse to make a tsunami or anything large in a physical sense, but I could read the information all the particles gathered. But it was too much information. I would have to somehow learn to read only the important parts, but I did not know how yet.

The last event that put me together was when Senecus took and used Odin's gifts. Just like Jo's pregnancy, that shocked my entity inside Senecus into full sentience. Enhanced and energized, I knew it was time to separate from him. Leaving my essence behind, the sentient portion of me left his body and returned to the waters. My imbued DNA from the water began to come to me, and I became something new, similar to what had happened with Jo, but with a resemblance to a human male.

My two entities patterned on the two humans found each other in the water and melded. I was now me, whatever me was. A hybrid sentient, not physical, not ascended, yet both.

I sensed other versions of me begin created a short distance away. I called to them and as they left their hosts, leaving them with the essence, they traveled to me through the water, and we joined together. I was getting less amorphous and much stronger as a sentient being. I realized from those new forms joining me that their hosts were the humans I had tried to help some time ago, and they called themselves fae. The cycle was finally completing itself. As more of my versions formed, I let them stay unassimilated. They coalesced together and formed more versions of me, but separate, as cloned sisters. For the first time in 60 million years, I had others of my people, a new people, to converse with.

Meanwhile I felt the alien presence that had planted the bad virus return, then take Jo back to their time. I felt them physically rip my remaining essence from her during their torture procedures. Their mistake was doing that in a room not sealed or sterilized. My essence diffused into the water vapor in the room, and then coalesced once out of the room and in a water source. Similar to before, my particles began rapidly multiplying. Because of my experience, I can manage and guide the process from this Earth time and place via quantum entanglement. It will take time, but I shall assert my presence when mature, and those evil beings will realize my wrath.

My consciousness stayed close to Isabel to provide any support that I could, also to protect her if anyone came for her. I still maintained some distance as I could not let her imprint me. I made sure she knew Jo was her mother and that I would always be with her, but more distantly as a grandmother.

I found I could manipulate water to make new forms, including advanced crystals. After creating them I could congregate my consciousness into them and create powerful data nodes. All my memories plus the millions of years of data from all my DNA particles floating in, around, and through the planet. More of my consciousness began reading all the data and forming patterns. I placed crystals around the planet, including Lake Baikal, the Irish channel, and several other locations. I wanted to place one in Lake Superior but crystals in the area were too hostile.

An awareness came to me of the smoke demons, the remnants of a few of my people that refused to leave Earth after ascension. Now they were insane, and I suppose it was proof that my way of survival was better. But it was a very near thing.

I've been reacquainting myself with the initial entities and Guardian species that my people engineered and left here, along with some of those associated with but not part of the fae. I was surprised that a number still exist, such as Odin, the one known as Fate and many more. I'm also aware of many that are much less friendly and are going to pose a serious threat to humans. They will need to be watched and dealt with.

My grand experiment, and my own survival, finally proved successful after sixty-five million years. But it is not over. There is still much to do.

Chapter Eighteen

College

I had always been interested in what caused my condition. There was not much if any information available to study, so I muddled around for a few centuries just existing and surviving after my transformation. But my curiosity kept me searching for clues. The Church archives in Rome were a likely place to start, but I believed that I'd meet a quick death if they realized that I was not exactly human. The next best place to look were the universities. Enough odd people already congregated in their halls, so I would not be out of place. That began my part-time career as a serial university student.

Of course, almost everything I learned turned out to be useless or wrong. But in other ways, including learning how to interact with normal humans, females, and administrators, it was worthwhile. And yes, I considered those groups as species separate from me. My time as a student was also some of the most normal years of my life since my transformation. I was just another student and rarely had to use my advanced skills to throttle another student or professor. Although a few sexual predators did find their hobby curtailed via crushed testicles once I learned of their proclivity.

I spent one university stint learning medicine and anatomy, another on the science behind European folklore and supernatural beings, a fun degree on fish proteins, a third dissertation on the microbiology of mud from a certain river in Holland, and yet another on human virology. The last and relatively recent degree was on the human microbiome. That was probably the only one that applied to my condition. I also deviated from the life sciences and did a degree in archaeology at Leiden. It was just a lark at first to see how much they had dug up, literally, in the Roman period in old Holland. There was a definite lack of documentation and significant loss of content that had happened over the centuries. I found no reference to myself. My life, soldier's career and passing out of history was never noted. Not that I expected to find anything. However, vanishing with no mention in history hurts the ego. Individuals listed as missing from the Legion were common enough, but that looked bad for the commanding officers and the patron, so most missing soldiers were listed as lost to disease or accident, or just disappeared from the roles.

Students in the old universities were male, rowdy, oversexed, and bored. Although most of those conditions still apply at most institutions. Young men with little to do but drink and carouse after classes. Even some of the professors would wander into the local taverns. Each town profited from the rented rooms, prostitutes, and alcohol. The towns also learned to suffer various outrages from all those bored students.

My first stint as a student was at Padua University in northern Italy. Padua was a small but ancient town, and is worth visiting today, albeit much larger. Because it was one of the earliest European schools to offer studies in medicine and anatomy it was a natural place for me to study. For a couple of centuries, it was the leading medical school in Europe. The program was ahead of most of Europe because it offered anatomy and dissection of human bodies. Padua and its university were far enough from Rome to escape Church scrutiny, and the takeover of the region by Venice kept a secular slant on such study. Much of the rest of Europe was restricted from using human cadavers by religious edict. At Padua, the dissections were quite useful for studying basic anatomy and physiology, but some of the explanations cooked up by a few of the professors regarding organ functions were ludicrous. But I needed as much data as possible to search for the reasons of my condition, so I enrolled.

I found that Padua was a pleasant place in the warmer months but could be brutal in the winter. Student rooms were small, dark and cold. The only recourse was for all the male students to pile into the taverns after class. Even that proved tedious as the cold months dragged on. But then a weather event brought a heavy snowfall followed by sunny days without frigid temperatures. Students being students, another outlet was found for all the pent-up energy.

My story begins with a beautiful snowfall but ends rather badly with body parts. But in between it was a hell of a lot of fun.

The snowball fight between medical and theology students occupying different buildings seemed inevitable. The buildings were separated by a green swale filled with small trees and bushes that bloomed in the spring. It was a tiny yet unplanned park. Horses were not allowed so the paths were clear of mud.

Now a beautiful snow covered the terrain. Nice, packable snow, perfect for balling up and throwing. Easy to access for two groups of students already at odds with each other based on fields of study, although most of our confrontations were friendly.

The snowball fight began and lasted for a solid week. As the snow melted, passions did not, so we began raiding the local bakeries and stealing baskets of small breads and buns. Once stale they made adequate projectiles without causing any harm. Of course, we as science students looked for an edge in the great bread fight. Slipping a small rock into the middle of the loaf added a bit of distance and impact. Force equals mass times acceleration, even in a rock-laden bun. A day later, the pummeled theology students responded in kind, and the battle intensified, as most of us began skipping classes to plan ambushes and skirmishes.

Professors began noticing absences, and the local bakers complained to the administration about purloined breads. But what ended the affair was the introduction of body parts as projectiles.

It was a brilliant tactic. As we found out later, the theology students, knowing that we had access to anatomy classes, deduced that if they pilfered parts and pummeled the locals then we would be blamed. And they were right.

The next evening, just as two professors walked the path between the buildings, they noticed the abundance of baked goods in the melting snow. It was difficult not to, as dozens of crows had descended on the park and made a massive racket as they absconded with beaks heavily laden with muddy buns.

Then the professors were hit with portions of human hands, kidneys, and one genital. Their surprise was only exceeded by their outrage. They stormed off straight to the administrators. Within an hour, two administrators, the outraged professors, and members of the local police force arrived. After a quick and completely clueless investigation, they determined that the medical students were responsible; our immediate punishment was to clean the park of all breads and body parts, and the matter was never to be spoken of again. I believe the last part was to protect the administrators more than anything. That evening we all met in the nearest tavern, and the theology students bought us all a round. A lot of laughs and good-natured boasts followed. That ended the Great Snowball, Rock, Bread, and Body-Part War of Padua.

* * *

When I was enrolled at the University of Edinburgh, I ended up socializing with a small group of engineering students. They were all from Scotland and had spent some years together at the university. There was a final class they needed before they went out into the world and began their careers practicing all the nonsense they had leaned in college. The class was required but all the students put off taking it until the end of their academic career. The simple reason was that the professor was an ogre, the very worst representative of professors and their caricatures. Describing him as a combination of bigot, misogynist, classicist, and complete narcissist would only begin to detail the man.

My group of friends dreaded it, but they had no choice but to take the course to graduate. In a monumentally stupid decision based on drinking, peer pressure, and a bet, plus what could only have been black magic, I also signed up for the class. The bet was that I had to enroll and pass the class. If I won, the group would host a feast for me after graduation, then they would parade around the campus naked later that night. If I lost, I hosted a party for them at the local pub, then I strolled naked across campus. Worst case I would pay for my friends' graduation party, then walk around naked, which did not bother me.

Since I was not an engineering student and did not need the class to finish my degree, I felt safe taking it. Besides, it would be interesting to learn about some civil engineering projects common in Holland, like bridges, locks, canals and dams. I was wrong on both counts.

Professor Clegg was possibly worse than his reputation. A Londoner, he had been trained there and then employed at several rail companies. He'd also done a stint in the Engineering Department at Glasgow. Now he was Edinburgh's prideful problem. Possibly the most arrogant ass north of Hadrian's Wall.

My strategy of blending into the back of the class as a non-major seemed to enrage him, and he made a daily point of picking me out for ridicule. It probably did not help that I sat silently with a dumb grin on my face every time he denigrated me. He was not picking only on me, as he did it to every student in class every day. Because of the high stakes involved in passing the class, all the other students had to take his crap, and some took it very personally. I suppose that as one of the leading authorities in the field, he felt it appropriate to insult every student in the class nearly daily. Perhaps he thought it would keep the Scottish provincials in their place.

My friends were devastated by the barrage of insults and verbal garbage from that arrogant ass. Some weeks into class, after many discussions and professions of premeditated murder, a plot was hatched. The next two weeks were spent planning. Plus surreptitious measurements of the target area and the assembly of detailed engineering drawings.

My classmate Andrew, with whom I had made the unfortunate bet, had an artistic girlfriend. Elizabeth, whom we called Bethany, was in a different building and part of campus than us in science and engineering, but I thought her talents would be beneficial for our project. Andrew agreed and we talked to her about our project. We arranged for her to visit the area for which we needed assistance. Sketches were made and she left to start the fresco and I paid for all the supplies. Bethany later claimed it was her first commissioned work. She and Andrew did not remain a couple after graduation. Rather than accept his proposal, she went on to become a successful set designer and worked at the major theaters in London.

Late at night a week later, we were ready, and the teams went to work. James and Hamish set off for Professor Clegg's house. Robert and Monty went to the building and began preparations. Andrew picked up the package from Bethany and met me a half block from the building in a dark alley. We waited there for James and Hamish, then escorted them to the building with the project. At the door we went into a fast mode of disassembly based on the plans drawn up beforehand. Ten minutes later, with Robert and Monty's help, the entire project was in the building.

We hung Bethany's artwork in the hall to mask our activities, as we knew the night watchman sometimes looked in the window set in the door on his rounds. Bethany's fresco was the empty hallway at night. It would not stand scrutiny, but we knew the oft-inebriated watchman would not know the difference. The six of us reassembled the project in twenty minutes, then we made some safety preparations and left.

The next morning was the most anticipated day of the year for us. An already irate Professor Clegg arrived to find his prized carriage and horse occupying the hallway directly in front of our classroom. He was mad and late as he could not find his transportation that morning, obviously. He was apoplectic at the sight in the building. The smell did not help either. We had left the horse a partial bucket of grain and a full bucket of water. No reason for him to suffer, plus we wanted him to be completely full and to continue working his digestive and excretory systems while in the hallway. It was fitting to give back what had so freely been tossed at us by Professor Clegg.

After screaming for two minutes, he got even madder when he realized no one was going to help him remove the horse and carriage from the hallway. Not that the carriage would have fit through the doors. That became apparent when he finally paid some workers to fetch his carriage. It was poor planning on his part, not having detailed drawings of his own carriage. Nor did we offer them up. The workers sawed the cart into three pieces, destroying it, but luckily the horse did fit through the doors.

Our work was done. To celebrate we all walked around naked on campus one night. We all managed to keep quiet until graduation, but shortly afterward the word got out and the group became something of campus heroes. Anyone from our group that visited the campus the following couple of years never had to buy a drink in the taverns. Unfortunately, not long after that, three of our group perished in Europe. World War I came calling, and killing, and from 1915 to 1918, and my friends died. As did millions of others. Altogether it was an enormous waste of talented humanity.

* * *

I met a young woman during my studies in Leiden that neatly sliced through my life like a cutter in a rough sea. Or more like a meat cleaver slamming through a chicken carcass. I, chicken; she, cleaver. No, it was not that dramatic, and it did not affect me to the extent just mentioned. But it was the type of promo she would have written for her commercial, as an overly dramatic marketing major. But it was mostly good fun, regardless of her intent.

Meeting women during my university sojourns was easy but choosing an appropriate one was more difficult. Even more so for me, as I preferred a smart, attractive female that wanted an attachment somewhere between a two months and two years, with no chance of lasting longer or marriage ever rearing its ugly head. Imagine having that conversation on the first date; it rapidly led to no further dates. But after trial and error I developed a better sense of the type I needed to make it work. Caring enough to have a relationship, but sadistic enough to push those spiked heels through a naked back when the time was right.

It was an exciting time in Leiden and I found an exciting, petite American blonde with a cutting edge. Marilyn had spent a lot of time in the Netherlands and Europe because of her father's business interests, so we had plenty to talk about. She was studying marketing, and I was sure she would end up in her daddy's business. She always denied it. But he had engineered her life around that very thing. Since I was mature enough to know how to not say certain things, I did not say them.

The first year was good as they typically are. Lots of sex, movies, lectures, cafes, and sitting by the fire in the long blustery winters. Bike riding and canal boating in the warm months, with more cafes and picnics when the clouds allowed. Good times like that rarely last. Lots of togetherness and tenderness in the first months, slowly wearing toward little fights and my noticing her glances at other gentleman in the cafes and clubs. Those shanks of hers were rusty and needed some new blood.

At the beginning of our second year together, I opened the

door to her place, which we shared part-time, as I still had my own place. She walked out of the bedroom naked and with a sheen of sweat, and a large, good looking, dark-haired guy followed her out. He was naked, too. Sheeny as well.

She glanced at me. "Meet Jorge. He's new, and he is staying. I don't think that you are." Jorge was hovering just behind her and had a smirk on his face but said nothing. Another fellow, blonde and naked, walked out and stood to the other side of and behind Marilyn. He at least had the sense to have a confused and embarrassed look on his face as he grabbed a towel.

"This is Nils," she said.

I nodded to the blonde guy. "Man, you guys started partying without me," I said. "Now I'm going to have to play catchup. Who has the lube?"

Jorge lost his smirk. Nils looked more confused.

"No, remember, you are not staying," Marilyn said. "Don't be so obtuse. The party's over and I'm done, at least for now. Then me and the boys will complete another round of business."

"Yeah, I can see your business, and it looks crowded. I'll go."

I could have coldcocked – who says I can't pull a pun – both of them in a couple of seconds, and then tweaked the little vixen's nose in a loving embrace. But I was just done, and she was not worth the effort. Besides, I knew what I was getting into at the very beginning of the relationship. Now I had gotten it, although it was still bittersweet to end like this. But she was a marketing major, and I figured this was her first commercial; this was her "making a statement." Daddy would be proud of his little Monstress.

"Anyway, I am late for the orgy over at Lisbeth's, so I'll pick up supplies on the way," I said. "You guys need to get back at it, looks like shrinkage is setting in." Marilyn's haughty look turned surprised for a second as I turned and left through the door, which I didn't close.

I did not see her again as we did not share any classes, and the campus and town were large enough to avoid each other. Years later I thought of her, and the miracle or curse of the internet allowed me to look her up. She had had a rising career in dad's company in New Jersey until he died, and the company went belly up. Her last address was in the Atlanta suburbs. The only other information I found was that she had a couple of grown kids, at least three divorces, and had retired from a mundane job. I knew nothing about her actual life but assumed she had kept making dramatic commercials for each of her husbands as they in turn became exes.

I have dozens of stories about universities, professors, and fellow students. Many of them are quite entertaining. But most of them will remain untold and slip into the anonymous history that most tales meet after our passing. I suspect the same is true for almost the entirety of human experience, except for those few stories that get written down.

Chapter Nineteen

Dogs

Late one night, I got a surprise call from Monk.

"I have found a predator here in The Netherlands. Specifically in Utrecht, where I have the location down to the block, and likely to the house."

"Impressive. You can't have been running the program very long."

"I modified the second model again and added new parameters. I hypothesized that the predator algorithm would work with enough good data for other applications. Ultimately, the location, species, or time frame is irrelevant. Expanding it showed many new correlations, everything from unscrupulous business practices to this unusual case in Utrecht."

"OK, but I don't recognize lots of humans disappearing in Utrecht. Or are they being brought in from elsewhere?"

"It's not humans. The missing victims are dogs."

"What?"

"I have run and rerun the program, and a particular residence stands out in Utrecht that is responsible for missing dogs. Because we have no stray dogs in The Netherlands, the algorithm picked up the nexus easily."

"Huh, did not see that coming. How did you get it so specific to find the exact house?"

"The program gave me an approximate location. Further investigation pointed to the exact house."

"And what was that evidence?"

"The same woman has been living in that house for centuries, at least since 1674. The Great Storm destroyed records prior to that time, but I aspect she was there before then."

"What? The same woman?"

"There must be an echo on the line, or you have become decrepit. Yes, same name, and same signature on the property records."

"Damn. I went to great lengths for many years to pass my property to myself, cover my tracks, and a woman in Utrecht sits there for nearly four hundred years and nobody even notices."

"Of course no one notices. If she pays her taxes and does not get into trouble, why should the government care, even if she is four hundred years old? That isn't a crime."

"Oh, wow, I just don't know how to respond. But that is another thing to like about The Netherlands. Nobody gets into your business. Even to check up to see there is an immortal in town."

"I also drove by. It is an immaculate place and has been well kept. If you need to dispose of her, please let me know. I would be interested in buying the house and moving to Utrecht. This body is too hot to be confined to a small town like Gouda."

"Monk, you continue to surprise me. But you are always practical. Can you send me the report?"

"Certainly. And this one is free, as it was a systems test."

"Sure. I don't suppose you were running the model for other pursuits, such as searching for royal daughters of marrying age?"

"Of course I was, but with different modifications. Those mods must be in error, as the model shows no matches. I've expanded the search again beyond royalty. I am certain I can find someone appropriate."

"Good luck with that dating search. I'll talk to you later."

What the hell could I do about an immortal dognapper? Was it even a crime? And where did all the dogs go? I knew some dogs were sold into laboratory research in the past, others to those despicable dog fighting groups, or even breeding farms. But someone that old probably wasn't into any of those things. Then again, she obviously wasn't trying very hard to hide. Very curious.

I made time for a trip back to Utrecht. The house really was immaculate, so Monk had good taste, even if his desire was misplaced. Old style but updated and what looked to be all modern conveniences. The front garden was something from a magazine. I opened the gate, then knocked on the front door.

A woman that looked to be in her mid to late fifties opened the door. She was beautiful and somehow matched her house. I got witch vibes from the situation.

"Good morning. May I help you?" she asked in Dutch.

"Hello, I am inquiring about Maria," I answered in English.

"I am Maria."

"Hi Maria, my name is Senecus. I came by to ask you about missing dogs."

"I don't know what you mean. I have seen no dogs about today."

"Well, it's just not about a dog missing today. More about the last four hundred years, all the time you have been living here."

She kept her composure well. "I'm sure I do not know what you mean."

"I think you do. Maria, I am not here in any official capacity, nor are you in any trouble. I am an old, old neighbor from Woerden. From the Roman garrison days, in fact. But you have now appeared in a database that has come to my attention, so I must inquire about the dogs. I also have the ability and resources to provide help if you need any. There is no threat to you in this inquiry."

She looked conflicted, and I thought she was about to close the door. Then she looked at me. "Would you like to come in for a cup of tea? Perhaps we can clear this up."

"Thank you."

I stepped into the house, which was as nice on the inside as on the outside. Through the windows, I saw the back gardens were even more lush than the front.

"You say that you were nearby in Woerden and in the garrison. How did you survive the madness that killed nearly everyone?"

"Well, I think that question confirms my thought that you have been here longer than four hundred years. A representative of the Church inoculated me on the night of that outbreak, as part of a force to fight the vampires. But in my case, something else happened, and I missed the battles. Much later I came back through this region, and even helped to build the Dom tower. I moved on to other places including America, but still keep homes here. So that is a brief history of me; how did you come to be in Utrecht?"

"Many, many centuries ago, my small family lived in a village just over the Pyrenees Mountains, in northern Spain. My father felt it necessary to leave, and we made our way across France and Belgium. It took years, so we came to this area just as the madness that killed the Legions was ending. So many people had died. My father saw an opportunity to settle where no one knew us or would persecute us. Here we stayed for more centuries, as my parents died, then my older brother. I stayed because I did not know where else to go, and I don't think we had any distant family left in Spain, as we had cut all ties there. I made my life here, such as it is, and though the people were suspicious, they have left me alone. Even the French, and later the Germans, did not bother me."

"I'm sure then that you are older than I. But we both have seen many years pass in this place. Does anything in your history explain the missing dogs?"

"It is a great shame for us, and the reason we kept moving. Yes, the dogs have always had a dominant influence on us. My people are very ancient, but for some unknown reason, we require dogs to live. We must... extract... certain tissues from them that unfortunately leaves them lifeless. Because of that, in old times, people considered us cursed, and sent us away. Over time, especially recently, the taking of a dog's life is taboo. I feel terrible every time I do it, but otherwise I fall ill, and instead of dying I feel terrible pain and shrink up. I don't seem to be able to take my own life as nothing has worked so far."

"I have not heard of that condition before, but it is hardly surprising, considering all the different species and specific needs in nature."

"True, but it is still a shame, I bear. I have tried many ways around it, trying extracts from other species, removing samples from deceased dogs, and funding research at universities to produce a supplement. Nothing has worked."

"What materials are you extracting?"

"The top of the brain stem and the glands in the brain. And it must be extremely fresh."

"Yes, I see how that prevents most other solutions."

"It has been a severe problem, and it has gotten worse. Few missed stray dogs fifty years ago, but now a missing dog can turn into an investigation."

"How do you dispose of so many bodies?"

"Have you noticed my gardens?"

"Ah yes, lovely. I suppose they are well fertilized."

"Yes, but because I know what lies beneath, they bring me little joy."

"From what other species have you tried to extract your needed ingredients?"

"Most everything related to dogs that was available, plus many mammals. An old story I heard as a child said our grandfather even tried a human. I'm sure that was another reason we were ostracized. A few years ago, I even tried one of the deer at the local park. But the proteins or enzymes or whatever chemicals we need are not present."

"Have you thought about moving?"

"Many times, but I don't know where to go. Europe is mostly closed to me because stray dogs are not common, and America scares me too much. If they catch me and put me in jail, I will fall into a terrible illness. But even then I would not die, but turn into a husk full of pain. The only positive thing I've noticed is that, as my life tapers off from age, I need fewer dogs to survive."

"That should help then, as fewer dogs disappearing equals less risk for you. How is your Spanish?"

"Rusty, but I go to the Spanish restaurants here and talk to the owners. I can pick it up quickly once I talk. But Spain is not open to me for the reasons I've mentioned."

"I understand. But I am thinking of a country that I have visited, with weather much like Spain, with Spanish language, beautiful countryside, very nice and affordable houses with sprawling courtyards, and many stray dogs."

"That sounds quite attractive. Where is this place?"

I told her where it was, and all the details I could remember. She was interested enough to start her own research. It was all I could do for now.

A few years later, I stepped out of the links, near an airport car rental office. I drove to Villaflores, a cute town in Chiapas, Mexico. It was about as far down in Mexico as you could get without being in Guatemala or the Pacific Ocean. I pulled up to a house in town and entered the building into a courtyard that was full of plants, from beds of flowers to medium trees. One portion was open to the sun, and in another section there was a large, covered area. Shade plants held reign there, and the cover provided shelter during the rainy season. Furniture was scattered across both living areas outside. It was a living courtyard instead of a living room. There were large glass doors to close off part of the house for the few days a year when it was too cold or too hot for the courtyard.

Maria greeted me there with a tray of refreshments. We exchanged pleasantries, but it was brief, as we still did not know each other that well.

"I'm glad this has worked out for you. You seem to have settled in nicely here. I saw lots of stray dogs as I drove in, so things have changed very little here."

"There are many dogs, but perhaps a few less than before. Yes, my life here is better than it was in Utrecht. I have enjoyed it immensely, and it is a good place for me."

"That is good to hear. Then you have had no problems?"

"None, other than the guilt that follows me for what I do. I try to assuage it by giving to the animal shelter, volunteering at the schools, giving money and buying books for them, and supporting the youth soccer teams. I am always busy and they have welcomed me here. How are you doing?"

I gave her the brief version, including my family life. Her face reflected that she was happy for me, yet still sad underneath. We sat in silence for a few moments.

"Senecus, you still seem troubled by my situation. But none of this is your fault. Tell me, why have you come?"

"I have been a little unsettled by your plight. I just didn't have any good ideas about how to fix this. But I am glad that you are happier here."

"Senecus, you just cannot fix some things. I love this place and its people. It reminds me of my hometown, but more vibrant. But I hunt and survive and give back to this community and I still cry after every dog. But recently I felt the turn, and I'll be gone in a few years, finally ending this curse. I'll leave my substantial assets to this place and its people. I thank you for helping me find my way and giving me a chance that few would have. So no, it's not fixed, but it worked out anyway."

"Maria, all those years in Utrecht, did you have a career or profession?"

"Most of that time I was a teacher, for younger children. It was one way to give back to the community. Why do you ask?"

"If there was a cure for your condition, would you be interested?"

"Yes, more than anything. But there are no solutions left, you know that."

"There is something new that might work. You could be free of your curse, but if worked it would add some years to your life. I'm not sure if that is your preference."

"I would try this thing you have. I don't mind the extra years if they are without the curse, and if I could be useful in some way."

"Good. First, drink this water."

She did. "Was this part of the cure?" she asked.

"Not exactly. It is more of an evaluation of whether the cure will work. It is also a test of your character, as we don't typically give out near-immortality to everyone."

A ghostly specter of a woman with rainbow hues appeared on the sofa next to us. It startled Maria at first, but the presence was soothing and surprisingly, Maria stayed where she was. Danu's aura gave an affirmative nod then faded away.

"Who or what was that? She was beautiful, and even though a ghost, I felt comforted."

"That was Danu, the goddess of water. Or that is what she is now. She confirmed the cure will work, and that you are a good person. I already thought so, but Danu confirmed it."

"Thank you. How does this work? And how can I ever repay you?"

"It may be better if you go back with me to our settlement in Danu Valley. The minor procedure will only take a few minutes, but in your case, we'd like to watch over you for a day or two. We can go today if you'd like."

"That sounds fine. I'll start packing for the trip and will ask a friend to take care of the house. But is it possible to get tickets so quickly for the flight?"

"Uh, well, we won't be flying conventionally."

I explained to Maria about how some of us traveled, and that it was safe. I also told her more about the Valley and our people.

"It sounds lovely," she said. "I look forward to seeing it and meeting everyone."

"Oh, Maria, you asked about repayment. We require nothing from you for this. You are welcome to remain here, move to Danu Valley, or spend your time in both places. But that is not a decision you need to make anytime soon. Yet if you like the Valley, we are always looking for teachers. After you visit and have time to think about it, we'd welcome you as a teacher."

"That also sounds wonderful. Can we leave now?"

Maria came to Danu Valley and never really left. She kept her house in Mexico and ended up using it as place for Danu Valley students to visit and study in Mexico and Central America. She also established the house and grounds as a dog sanctuary, and it is the most successful facility in Mexico. Meanwhile, she became a fixture in our community and a beloved teacher.

Chapter Twenty

Date Night I

Nick

My gorgeous wife Sarah came into the room. Or maybe soon-to-be wife, if I passed the parent test in this European registered-partner system. She looked good even though she was tired as a new mom of twins. I was a new dad and tired as well, but not enough to miss a chance to admire her. Few knew that underneath that wondrous human surface she was a wolf. Fortunately, I was too. That meant we could do dog-style like few couples could. But I had learned that saying it out loud in her presence earned me a sharp elbow.

"How's Romulus and Remus?" I asked.

"Oh god, don't start that again."

"Well, it was kind of funny. Or was the first time."

"Must be a man thing. Of course, Senecus would say those names since he's a two-thousand-year-old Roman. But you didn't have to laugh at it or repeat it."

"I know. I won't bring it up again."

"Thanks. You should remember Jo elbowed him in the stomach when he said it."

"Yeah, that must be a woman thing since you do it to me too. Or is it British?"

"Doesn't matter. But if you men-children behaved better your ribs wouldn't be tender. Anyway, next feeding is your turn."

"Sure thing. Are we still on for the Ireland trip?

"Yes, Morrigan said she still needs us. Hopefully no more of the boring court stuff. We need something exciting to work on."

"Hey now, watch out. Those could be famous last words with that bunch of fae."

"True. But now I have you to protect me since I'm so fragile."

"Hah, you best me nearly every work out. Give a woman the Danu essence and she turns into a monster."

"Monster, huh?" Sarah's eyes flashed hard, but with a glint of humor.

"Uh, yeah, but in a good way. A very good way. Good looking momma monster kind of way."

"Of course, I thought you'd come to that conclusion."

Sarah draped herself across me as I leaned back in the leather chair. We were often busy, but I really enjoyed these times when we bantered and then she sat on me in the chair. She just felt good and always smelled like chocolate and spices. Except when we ran in the rain together as wolves. Then we both came home smelling like, well, wet dog. But that was OK, because we got to shower together.

But my previous statement was true, however uncouth my wording. Quite a few men and women in Sen's group, plus many of the fae in Morrigan's group had taken the Danu essence. Although all greatly benefited, almost always the women gleaned more speed and power than the men. Among our group there was no longer any physical differences between the sexes. Except of course for the obvious. But that made things better for everyone as there was no inequality on the kickball field. Or anywhere else in Danu Valley.

"The plan for our babysitters still good?" I asked.

"Yes, mum and Henry can watch them for a couple of days. They must be gluttons for punishment. I'm not sure whether to have them come here or if we take the twins to the Valley."

"Any news of your father?"

Sarah grimaced. "Nothing recent. Morrigan's network spotted him in Russia and Chechnya a few weeks ago. Doing something illegal I'm sure."

"Hmm. I know how dangerous Henry is and how formidable your mom is, but maybe we should take the twins to the Valley just to be safe. She and Henry will be more comfortable in their own house anyway."

"Maybe you're right. I will be glad not worrying about something stupid my father might try."

I was not really worried regardless of which decision we made. I once thought of Henry as a distant cousin, then I pieced together that he was born during the last Ice Age and his lineage was vastly older than any ancestors of mine. And he'd spent a lot of that time as a Warden, or "hunter of bad guys" across Siberia and North America as the glaciers melted. Sarah's dad was not going to pose any problems for him. It paid to know people with special abilities. But, like any parent, I wasn't willing to take any chances. Off to Danu Valley we would go, the safest place in the known world. Although it was not quite in this world. It also was an easy choice since we could travel those six thousand miles in a second. We'd drop the kids off in the time bubble that protected Danu Valley in the far west of North America, then a second later we'd be in Ireland. The only downside was the lack of frequent flyer miles. But well worth it since we never had to partake in the disaster that was air travel.

"Hey, since they can take the twins for two days, maybe we can do a date night in Ireland, then have Kal meet us for that project we are supposed to be working on."

"Yes, that might work. We should ask Kal if he is available."

"I'll ask him when we get to the Valley."

Sarah and I wore our good clothes for the next evening. As members of Morrigan's court we felt it appropriate to dress well. All the items for the twins' needs were packed up in a large bag along with the oversized stroller. Henry popped into our back courtyard, then blinked us back to Danu Valley. Landing in the village green, we walked to their house. Elizabeth, Sarah's mom, and Henry had been an item for a while. It was good to see Elizabeth enjoying life after her past health and marital problems. We chatted with Elizabeth and Henry and passed over what seemed like a hundred pounds of baby supplies.

Henry delivered us to the front lawn of the designated country estate in Ireland. He checked the surroundings for any threats, then he blinked away. We entered the house and Seneschal greeted us personally before we went to the head table. He remained and greeted each additional guest. It was not obvious, but I wondered if he was checking for threats before any of us met Morrigan. Once again, I wondered if he was something much more than an advisor. Morrigan had more enemies than most among the fae, and she had survived so far. Perhaps she had good help.

We sat at the big kahunas table like the royalty we apparently were now. Sarah and I still laughed at the bizarre manner we went from being absolute nobodies to nobles of the fae court. Oh well, we were not getting paid or getting anything else for our troubles, but at least Morrigan fed us well.

There were rounds of small talk as the banquet progressed, then Sarah and Morrigan entered a long conversation about strategy. I tuned out and talked with Seneschal as Sarah would brief me later. I tuned back in as I heard Morrigan suggesting we leave the banquet early and start our date night. Sarah must have told her the twins were out of the house for a couple of nights. Getting out of here early was all good with me.

"You and Nick should depart now and start your weekend

early," Morrigan said. "Have an evening out. Seneschal will lend a hand and steer you to a great place."

"I'd be happy to assist you two," Seneschal said.

The three if us left the table and went outside. He blinked us into town, somewhere in Galway near the river. He suggested a restaurant on that block, then left us to go back to the banquet. There happened to be a car sitting there and he had dropped the keys in Sarah's hand before he blinked out, because he had heard how bad I was at driving on the wrong side of the road.

The restaurant was small but seemed nice inside. A small woman greeted us, and we sat and ordered drinks. I saw someone in the back, but that was all. Apparently, it was a two-person operation.

The woman had delivered our drinks, stood there with an odd look on her face, then walked out the front door. We were digesting that and wondering if it was a concern, when a large something walked out from the back of the place. Massive legs, wearing pants, but a literal bull from waist up – huge shoulders, neck, short horns, everything but a ring through the nose.

In a deadpan voice, Sarah asked, "Nick, did you order a rare steak?"

The only other couple in the restaurant took one look at the thing, squawked, and ran out as fast as possible. I thought about the great dress Sarah was wearing, an emerald green silk number that match her eyes and complemented her hair. I thought about my expensive charcoal wool suit. Sarah looked at me and I knew she was thinking the same thing. Those clothes were about to be a total loss.

"Think Morrigan is good for the new clothes?" I asked.

"Sure, but afterwards it could be a little embarrassing when we walk around town nude."

"Nah, I know where we can get some leather clothes. May not be cured out but we can still make a couple of capes out of him."

The bull didn't appear amused. Cows are like that sometimes.

"It's not what you think," he said.

Sarah and I looked at each other and burst out laughing at the sheer absurdity of the situation and that statement. We both dropped a little into slant to check for threats, but there was nothing imminent. Good thing as we wouldn't have to burst into wolf form, shred our clothes, and bring down this half-bovine giant. We relaxed, just a little.

"I'm Bill," he said. "Siobhan, the hostess, is a seer, and picked up on something. She let me know trouble was coming. She went around back to watch. Probably best as she is not much good in a fight."

"It's interesting we would end up having dinner in a place like this," Sarah said.

"Seneschal would only send you to some place he feels would be safe. He has let it be known throughout the realm that you two are to be taken care of, regardless of where you travel. We will endeavor to keep you safe."

I thought of the last time I'd heard a minotaur standing in an Irish restaurant using the word endeavor. Nope, I was right, this had never happened before. The three of us went out the front, and I thought about the car up the block. But that was not going to happen.

A small black sedan came fast down the street toward us. Bill turned and immediately ran straight at it. They met in a tremendous crash, and I figured we had seen the last of Bill. But remarkably, the impact left him on his feet, and he was only thrown ten feet back from the car. The car had fared much worse, with the front crumple zone tested to the limit. The driver and passenger were motionless behind the airbags, but there was some movement in the back seat.

"We should go. I'm good for head-on collisions but I'm not bulletproof. Take that paved path south along the river. I'll lead the survivors north for a bit, then double back and meet you at the next bridge. Unless you can portal out, or as you say, travel the links?"

Sarah and I looked at each other sheepishly. "No, we started training but have not mastered that," Sarah said. We would have to rectify that soon.

"When we meet up I'll take you to someone that can send you away from here. If I'm not at the bridge in fifteen minutes, then walk back into town to the Hardiman Hotel and ask for Vishnu. He will help."

"Thanks Bill."

"Good luck." He raced off north past the crumpled car as the two men in the back seat staggered out. Sarah and I entered the path along the river. It had bushes and trees alongside giving us some cover.

"Sarah, do you think this is your father's gig?"

"Those men looked burly, bald, and long-bearded. I saw tattoos on their necks, so I'd guess Chechen. Since he's been there lately these goons are probably another of his bad ideas. I doubt Morrigan will overlook this transgression."

"What do you think their plan is?"

"Father probably wants to kidnap me, then hold me for a ransom from Morrigan."

"Does Morrigan ever negotiate or pay ransoms?

"No, never"

"Glad you got your smarts from your mom." That earned me a quick smile. "What about me?"

"Father dislikes you so much that he'd probably have them catch you so they can torture you to death."

"Huh, in-laws. A good son-in-law is never appreciated."

"You did break his wrist and nearly rip out his throat in one of the most embarrassing displays at the fae court in a century."

"Yeah, I guess he holds a grudge."

We trotted down the paved but narrow path. I heard a pfft as something hit me in the back with a sting. Sarah was instantly aware and sidestepped another dart meant for her. We immediately faded backward into the bushes, then started moving as fast as possible parallel to the path.

"I was wondering when the other part of the trap was going to snap," Sarah said.

"Yeah, maybe the operation isn't as dumb as that first batch of goons made it look."

"Makes sense. They were just going to herd us if they couldn't take us. There was no room for us in that small sedan anyway, so there must be others about. And having a sniper was another good backup."

"You are brilliant. I sometimes forget that when looking at-"

"Are you smart enough not to finish that sentence?"

"Surprisingly, I am. Oh, this stuff in the dart feels like a big dose of ketamine."

"How the hell do you know that?"

"I once did a project developing an exoskeleton brace for people coming out of knee replacement surgery. A colleague wanted to try a smaller prototype on a pig before we fitted humans, to check on fitment issues. I don't like animal research, but it seemed like a good idea since the pig was not to be harmed. To keep the pig calm during fitting, though, my colleague decided to give it a shot of ketamine for both the pig's and our safety. I believe you should not do something to an animal you aren't willing to do yourself, so I had him give me a shot of ketamine beforehand."

"You might be crazy, but I like your thought process."

"Well, you did marry me. But my legs are feeling numb, so we better hurry before you have to carry me. And just ignore anything I say beginning in three minutes. And although unconscious, my eyes may stay open. It's eerie but normal."

"Great, an unconscious lug with open eyes spouting nonsense."

"Don't worry, it will be like a date at a university party."

"I don't know what kind of parties you went to, but that doesn't sound like any I attended."

I gave her the "I don't believe it" stare. "At least I've had the Danu essence so I should not be out more than a couple of minutes. Throw me under a bush if I get too heavy."

"Now those are more the types of parties I frequented."

Sarah must have followed my advice. I woke up under a massive yew bush. I calculated I'd been out for four or five minutes. I needed to ask Sen if there was a faster way to counteract chemical agents. I knew that he could, and I now needed that knowledge if I was playing high stakes games with the fae.

I heard a rustle and saw Sarah bending down to check me.

"Hi dear. Want to join me?"

"No time for that, get your lazy arse up. Bill is not around so we need to get the Hardiman."

I got up a little groggy but otherwise OK.

"What happened while I was out?"

"Another sedan showed up on the street through the shrubs. I disabled the two in it. Then I picked up a rock and slung it to where the sniper was hiding. I heard a thunk, then something heavy dropped off the roof, so I think that threat has been neutralized."

"Thanks. I'm glad you were busy while I was napping."

"Well, I can't always do all the work. Since you've been a slouch you get diaper duty all next week."

Chapter Twenty-One

Date Night II

Sarah

Nick and I ran a few blocks to the hotel near the transit station. There was a white van and another black sedan in the grassy park across the street, behind the hedge. I noticed it because a man that looked familiar walked up to the vehicles. He disappeared then reappeared with six men lying face down on the grass beside the vehicles.

"Uh Sarah, isn't that Seneschal?"

"I believe so. But after seeing that, I don't know what he is. No fae could do that."

"Glad he's on our side."

He looked up at us as we came upon the scene. "Ah, Lady Sarah and Count Nick, just the two I was expecting. Bill got tied up in traffic after ramming another car but told me you'd be arriving here soon. I took the liberty of disarming your welcoming committee."

"Thanks Seneschal," I said. "There are a few others scattered around back near the river.

"Quite right. I'll have my team gather them up and send them back where they came from. Good to see they didn't cause you any trouble. Good evening and enjoy your night."

A large van pulled up and Seneschal had a few words with the two fae that jumped out. He then disappeared as the fae loaded up the goons and sped off.

"Well, my sleeping beauty, looks like we have the rest of the evening off. Never say I don't provide an exciting date night."

"Excitement is good, but we should hang out with people that shoot at us less."

"Hey, it is not my fault you couldn't dodge a little dart."

"OK, but what should we do with our evening?"

"Let's go into the hotel since we are here, have a bite and a drink, then stroll back to our bed and breakfast."

"Sounds great."

The next morning, we hopped in the car left for us and I drove south a few kilometers past the Cliffs of Moher. Nick was atrocious at driving here as were most Americans. He did alright except for the high-speed roundabouts and narrow country lanes. We had to meet our friend Kal to explore the Irish coast in regard to a task requested by Morrigan. She wanted us to find a place and way to create a Danu Valley site, or find one already created. Apparently, there were legends that at least one site had been created and then lost. It sounded like a dubious pursuit, but we would comply with a cursory search.

At a small town down the coast, I pulled over at a car park overlooking the beach. A small man wearing a brown suit walked over and climbed into the back seat. I laughed because in reality the little fellow was nearly as big as the car and hairier than ten sheep.

"Hi Kal."

"Hello Sarah. Hello Nick. I trust you are both well? I saw your twins yesterday and they look to be healthy and happy."

"Yes, they are probably very happy getting spoiled by grandmum. But we are both well, thanks."

"Hi Kal, thanks for coming over," Nick said.

"Thank you for asking me over. I rarely visit this far, not because of the distance, but more of an unwritten policy that we don't encroach on this island. It already has enough issues with various factions claiming it as their own."

"Huh," Nick said. "I thought only the fae had laid claim to this land."

"They are the best known, yes, but there are others, some even older than the fae. But that is a tale for another time. I understand you are looking for a lost reserve somewhere along this coast?"

"Yes, there are legends about a land, a safe place long lost, somewhere along this stretch of Ireland," I said.

"I imagine there are remnants of fact in that legend, as there usually are with myths. If you would drive along, I will see what I can see." He laughed that very strange laugh at his pun.

I drove further south, taking roads directly along the coastline whenever possible. Kal sat quietly in the back seat with his eyes partly closed, his face always towards the water.

"Ah, Sarah, I think we can stop soon. There is something unusual nearby. Yes, park here if you can."

The three of us got out of the car. I did not see anything, and Nick looked over at me as he was thinking the same.

"Hmm, feels familiar. Please excuse me for a few moments while I converse with my people, then talk to the ancient ones that live here." Kal walked closer toward the ocean drop-off and sat on the ground and spread his large hands upon the grass. He had shed his human disguise and was back as a full-sized Bigfoot.

"What kind of ancients, Kal?" I asked, wondering if he could talk to ghosts.

"The moss, the lichens, the fungi. These or their clones are thousands of years old, or older, and they have genetic memory. Just takes a while to prod those memories as they don't process knowledge the way that we do." We waited a few minutes as Kal sat with his eyes closed. He sat a little longer, then stood up. "I have found it. We need to walk that direction a few hundred meters and closer to the cliff's edge."

We walked to another place on the cliff that looked like anyplace within miles of where we were. "Ah, it is as I thought. There is a haven here that was made by Merlin. Certain workings tend to be leave signs, and I felt Merlin's on this one. Let us see if we can find the doorway and enter. I know that he would not have made it easy to find or pass through."

We stood with Kal until he stepped to one side and even closer to the edge. "Here it is. I will go first, since if there is a trap or if I merely fall, I'll go into the links and be right back here."

He stepped to the cliff, leaped, and disappeared. A moment later he appeared as he leaped back toward us.

"Most interesting. It is not hidden in the way that I expected."

"I still don't see anything," Nick said.

"If you look straight out toward the ocean, do you see the slight haze?" Kal asked.

I looked and did see something, almost like a faint heat shimmer. "I think I see a shimmer or haze," I said.

"Yes, that is likely the effect from hiding the reserve but without the more elegant touches I expected. Almost anyone could accidentally jump off the cliff and enter. Not that most humans would jump off a perfectly good cliff. Sarah, do you know anything about this place?"

"Only that it has a reputation of being haunted, or considered bad luck. It is extremely stormy and ugly here, so most people avoid it."

"That might explain why it is not properly warded. Or this haven might manufacture bad weather as a passive defense. Regardless, you two can enter easily as there are no barriers or traps. Stand on that rock there and then jump forward as far as you can."

We did, but it was a harrowing leap of faith. Easier though as Kal could have caught us on the way down if needed and blinked us back to safety. My leap was about six feet. Any shorter and instinctively knew that I would not have made it and fallen. Without Kal, that would be over a hundred feet to the rocks and surf below.

We appeared onto what looked like a large island off the coast. There was a similar rock where we landed as to where we jumped from. This one had runes on it. Roughly translated, it said Coasthaven. I knew that because it glowed once I stepped on it and was able to read the runes. I just assumed it was some fae thing that would light up for anyone. Then I realized I could not read runes.

"How do I know that word?" I asked, out loud. "I don't know that language."

Kal turned around and studied me. He went quiet for a moment similar to how I'd seen him before when he queried the group mind of his people. They carried the total knowledge of the world for many centuries. Quite a trick that nobody else could perform.

"Ah, Sarah, I see now. Morrigan was correct in her assessment that your people are much more than they seem. That is why there are no active wards here. This place recognized you as the legitimate owner. The mark of Merlin is indeed on you and your people. I believe this is now your domain."

"Kal, this is not mine, I know nothing about it."

"But it knows you. In fact, I surmise that is was built for you, or your kind."

"That seems too crazy."

"Yet it is true."

"But didn't Merlin disappear before any of the work was done on the Maras, changing them from werewolves to fae? And how could he have then created this place and keyed it to us?"

"That is true, based on normal reality. My knowledge of Merlin was that he did not adhere to conventions. Nor did he obey the prohibition against interfering with time. He got around that by dabbling in the future but not going back and changing the past."

"That is hard to fathom."

"Yes, even for my people. We think he set up many useful things we have not found, at least not yet. Which I suspect was his plan all along. But while we are here, I suggest we take a quick look around. There could be other surprises."

We walked around for only fifteen minutes so did not get far from the entry point.

"It appears, perhaps, that it is unfinished somehow," Kal said.

"Is it safe to be here?" I asked.

"Yes, it is stable. But I'd rather not take too many chances since it is an unknown place."

All I saw as we walked was grass growing right up to the edge of the cliffs. I did not see any evidence of humans or animals, not even seagulls. I thought it a lovely setting though, and envisioned a cute two-story cottage with shutters sitting in the grass overlooking the water. A moment later, one sprang up from the ground, just as I had seen it in my mind.

Too shocked to say anything, I turned to look and Kal and Nick. They were just staring at me.

"I believe my earlier statement that you are the owner is corroborated by this evidence," Kal said.

Nick started smiling. "Guess we can skip the mortgage and building wait times if we move here."

"I really don't understand any of this. But I have to admit it is grand."

Kal suggested we depart. Before we left I looked back and the house still stood where I had imagined it into being. Very cool. We exited the same way we arrived, leaping from one rock to the other.

"With your permission, I would like to bring more of my people over to thoroughly check the physical presence of this haven before either of you spend much time here," Kal said.

"That is much appreciated, Kal. I might ask Danu to come back with me as well."

"That is eminently sensible. Please share this only with the people you trust. Goodbye, and we should talk soon to schedule my people."

We bid Kal goodbye as he blinked away. Nick and I moved back to the car to return to Galway.

"I suppose we should talk about how, or possibly if, we are going to tell Morrigan about this," Nick said.

"You don't trust her?" I asked.

"Not completely. Do you?"

"No, not yet. I know she is trying to be better, but she still has a long history of not always doing the right thing."

"How should we handle this? If Kal is right, this place might only be for you and your people."

"I'll let Kal's people check it first for safety. Then I think I shall bring Danu over for a look. I might ask her counsel about telling Morrigan. This place could be a boon to our people. But it could also be used for nefarious purposes."

"Seems sensible. If Kal is right and Merlin created it for you and the Maras clan, I'd say you have first right of ownership."

"But what does that mean?"

"The old saying of 'finder's keepers' might apply."

"Oh, thanks, that clears it right up."

"Sarah, you will figure it out. I'll be there to assist if Morrigan or anyone else doesn't like your decision."

"Good. Let's get back to the Galway B&B, it is time for high tea. And we still have tonight for ourselves."

"I'll second that."

The rest of our exciting weekend was slower, but nice. A quick blink to Danu Valley, then another back home to the Netherlands with the twins. I would talk to Danu soon, and before I saw Morrigan again. I had a secret to keep, apparently a large one.

Chapter Twenty-Two

Monk

I had a typical Dutch upbringing. Good parents, schools, and friends. My friends and I got into hacking rather than designer drugs or alcohol. I went to university in computer science mostly to learn cutting-edge cybersecurity, which I thought would make me a better hacker. I found that even self-taught hacking skills were more advanced than the traditional cybersecurity protocols. Hackers were almost always a few steps ahead. But I stayed to finish school because dropping out was so passé. Besides, there were more girls there, and as a computer guy I needed a larger pool to work with. Unfortunately, I graduated and went on to a most boring day job. Even more unfortunate, the professional women in the office had no interest in a young, handsome, brilliant man. Who was also humble. I slacked through the job and began serious hacking most of my free time.

My life as a hacker seems so far in the past. It was interesting at first, but then got boring. Hacking other people's work was so mundane. I needed more of a challenge than any company or government could provide. Then I met Senecus, and my work became very interesting and financially rewarding. Extremely rewarding, but sometimes dangerous. His projects kept me sharp and occasionally terrified. But then he asked to me to visit America, and my life transformed into something well past extraordinary.

I thought it was going to be a quiet vacation in a quaint valley in western America. All I knew about the area was from Hollywood movies. Maybe I would ride a horse for the first time, see a buffalo and chase cowgirls at bars selling swill water that passed for beer. Instead, I met something, or rather someone; a friendly Bigfoot named Kal. That was unexpected and definitely not in the old Westerns I knew from television. I also met a lovely woman that was a real Native American. Both changed me beyond belief, but unfortunately in my new trajectory, only one proved compatible with my future. It has been an interesting few years.

Now I am rock star in my field. A Dutch rock star, anyway. But as the saying goes, "if it ain't Dutch it ain't much." Lately I'm thinking that I alone am the field, as there in no person or company I can even consider as competition. I may have to leave the Netherlands and start my own country to house myself. But that would be lonely, so I'll need a queen to start the new monarchy. Preferably one that won't need too much of my time, other than for amorous activities. I should be able to afford someone like that with my newfound wealth.

How did I become the one and only real computer entity of the twenty-first century, bigger than all the others combined? A simple and cheap organic supercomputer. Simple for me at least, but too complex ever to be reverse-engineered. But I'm getting ahead of myself. Even contemplating such a system would have been impossible with my old mind.

Kal, the massive teddy bear, taught me a revolutionary way of thinking he calls slant. Learning it gave me the ability to exit the box, kick it down the street, run over it with a Maserati, and expand my limits to the size of a new continent. Or perhaps a new world, as I think my mind has expanded beyond most earthly limits.

My new and improved brain first thought to base a new

computer system on DNA. From long discussions with Sen and Kal, they though it unworkable. They summed it up best by relating that DNA was fantastic for data storage but would not work well as an operating system. A good model, but proteins would be too difficult to work with. Then Sen mentioned something about how a leaf had a three-dimensional network designed to get the most out of photosynthesis. That sparked an entirely new approach about moving away from a binary two-dimensional system and toward developing a quaternary three-dimensional system.

Sen's comment about the structure of a leaf got me to thinking of something I remembered from school, about eyes. Mainly, the structure of the retina, with multiple layers over sets of rods and cones. I decided a hybrid system using quaternary digits, or a base of four, when coded with color and organized into a three-dimensional system would far surpass the computational power of even the largest supercomputer. Incredibly complex, but I was just the person to make it work.

I designed it with four digits, four colors, and three dimensions, grown on a base of nanotubes. Then nanotubes were selectively removed, and the system was laid onto a printed carbon fiber membrane. That was carefully folded into thousands of folds per square centimeter as it was placed in a newly developed carbon gel. It really works somewhat like how proteins fold and unfold in cells based on information, but my nanoclusters communicate with different colors of light. A masterpiece of technology if I say so myself. Even better than DNA, both for data storage and operating systems.

Then I just had to tweak it to make it practical. And I did, with the help of slant to orient and train my nanoclusters. Plus, I used a lot of Sen's money to modify equipment and hire and train technicians to run the system to scale up production. My baby uses a fraction of the energy required by supercomputers with several magnitudes the computational power. It's also the size of a loaf of bread. But I will make it much smaller as that is the next project.

Sen never even wanted repayment. He said he just wanted a better computer. He got my first prototype, then he gave it back when he could not turn it off. The joke was on him, as I designed it without a power button. It is never off, so there was no reason for a button. I probably should have told him, but it was funny to watch him look for the phantom button.

But having a supercomputer half the size of a desktop was not enough progress for the new me. My first retail project was to design a near-super computer to carry in the pocket and replace smart phones. It was based on a much simpler and smaller spinoff of my supercomputer. It is a bifold computer where the front and back exterior covers are embedded with an ultrathin coating of solar panel collectors. Unfolding the computer, the screen is on the top flap and a keyboard is on the lower flap. Folded it is about the size of a passport, but even thinner at three millimeters. That item put most others out of business and made me my first hundred billion.

Another invention has been even better. After another epiphany, I combined a three-dimensional printer with a tattoo machine that was refitted with micronozzles. Then I modified and simplified the production process to make mini-supercomputer tattoos a few centimeters in length and width, and less than a millimeter thick. It runs off the body's excess heat and microcurrent. A tattoo about the size of a credit card, applied to the wrist, gives anyone a supercomputer that never turns off. The tattoo even has an antenna etched in it by a special conductive ink. The screen is also a new development better than any mechanical or digital screen.

There were technical issues involved in getting it to work on a human body, but Senecus brought in a guy I had seen around the Valley but didn't know. An excellent medical researcher by the name of Nick who happens to also be a wolf. When I found out he was living in the Netherlands we became close friends. Just as important, he got the tattoos to work without any problems with rejection or immune response. I made sure he got a nice percentage of the royalties; I really don't want a wolf mad at me. He also designed it so it can be removed just by pouring witch hazel on the wrist and the computer sloughs off.

Once again, Sen got the first tattoo, yet it was comical watching him peck away with one finger on his wrist. Slowly the people in the Valley got the tattoos, but as they traveled out in the world it has received a lot of notice. Michael's operatives were the first to adopt it outside the Valley, and now it will soon be offered to the world. Sen arranged for me the best intellectual property lawyers in Europe, which will keep the largest tech companies from copying it or co-opting it. Not that they could anyway. Each tattoo also has a kill switch embedded internally to keep it from being copied. Although I don't think anyone has the technology to even study it anyway.

Meanwhile, I have plans to travel to countries without resources or infrastructure and provide the tattoos for free. I hacked into satellites that others have already sent up so there is no shortage of signal. And if they give me any problems, I shall just take the satellites over and provide free service for everyone. Being a trillionaire gives even the billionaires pause. But it is important that information is never restricted.

Very early on I wasted time pitching my ideas to two of the larger companies in Silicon Valley. They professed no interest whatever. I realized they thought what I proposed was impossible. But even if there was the tiniest chance of success, they saw not a complement to their business model but rather a complete replacement. After that, I made sure they were right.

During the development of my products, I knew I had to find people to push through some of the early work. I had to provide designs that could be replicated, and work with some existing software applications and interfaces. I started looking at the largest companies in California. I quickly realized that the smartest people, especially if they are creative, do not work at large companies. I turned to recruiting at large universities, although I had my doubts, and my doubts were realized. I changed tactics and cast around coffee shops near small universities and colleges. Those were the places I had often hung out when in college. It was there that I found most of my people that came to form my company.

After a strange incident, I also discovered that other companies in the business would go to great effort to sabotage my project once they realized they could not steal it or reverse-engineer it. During the recruitment phase for people, I had a perfect candidate apply. Perhaps too perfect as even I thought something was odd. Through his own methods, Senecus found the candidate was a plant from one of the major companies. What did we do about that? We let him know that we knew, but by that time he had seen something of the project. He acted as a double agent for a month then completely left their service and joined us. He has been an excellent resource since that time. The best ideas, projects, and people generate an aura or field of loyalty and passion. Not even money can deter those on that path.

Anyhow, all my work life the past years has been good news. The sad portion of my life was also related to the development of the new computer systems and products. I realized that my new life, working twenty-hour days on my passion, left no room for other relationships. Including the one closest to me. Nan was the most important woman and partner I had ever met and lived with, but my work was my priority. I knew it hurt her, but she seemed to understand. We are still cordial and I still miss her sometimes. But I learned that despite my earlier interests in female companionship, my status is mostly unavailable.

Once I finish up current projects, however, I will revisit the option. Not with Nan, as she has found her true partner and is very happy. But there are still a few single European princesses out there, and now I have the vast wealth to impress one.

Although a woman I met last year in the Valley caught my interest. Sen introduced us and her name is Morrigan. I understand she is Irish so that helps. She looked a little young, but after much reflection, I have decided she is pretty enough for me. I'll ask Sen about setting us up on a date in a few months once my projects are finalized. If it goes well, perhaps we will progress to a long-term relationship. She could possibly my queen if I start that new country. But that kind of concept might scare her. Or my brilliance or incredible wealth might intimidate her. I'll need to proceed slowly, but I'm confident she will like me.

Chapter Twenty-Three

Christmas

I could tell Isabel was excited about the upcoming trip. What kid wouldn't be excited to go Christmas shopping in the fae realm underneath Ireland? I welcomed the trip too, but with some trepidation, which was wise when dealing with the fae.

Jo was clearly worried about going but hid it from Isabel. Not that it worked. Yet in a reverse manner, Isabel's positive excitement soothed Jo's fears. I was less worried about going since my wife was the premier warrior on the European continent, and our daughter was the best canary-in the-coal-mine trouble sensor that humanity had ever created. Isabel could detect any trouble at any distance, minutes before it manifested. I just had to be ready to react or tell Jo and let her beat any suspicious or threatening characters to a reasonable pulp.

The morning we were leaving, Jo came out wearing an elegant, form fitting grey cashmere dress with a cornflower blue overcoat to match her eyes. Her scarf carried most of the colors of the rainbow. She was visually stunning.

She looked at me as if I was not stunning. I thought my jeans and cotton sweater were fine. She shook her head and said, "Sorry dear, but that ensemble won't work. We are going to the land of the fae where we have a reputation already. I'm playing the game, presenting myself as an ally both dangerous and beautiful. It's about perception and the wielding of power as they see it. Silly as it is, we need to dress the part."

"I get it. What should I wear to complement you?" I ended up in grey slacks with a green cashmere sweater and charcoal overcoat with a silver scarf. The sweater and scarf matched my mismatched irises, one green and one silver, courtesy of Odin's gifts.

Before we left, Jo opened her coat to show to show me the two silver daggers hidden inside. Ever a resourceful girl. "I like the way you think," I said. "Also, the way you look." I grinned and opened my jacket to show her my "dress" tomahawk, smaller than my battle tomahawks, and fashioned with an ebony handle and silver head. She smiled back.

Isabel came out, we all held hands and I zapped us over to Ireland through the links. Isabel could have done it, but Jo was still uncomfortable with Isabel using her powers at such a young age.

It was our second shopping visit to the fae realm. Morrigan had control of most but not all the fae population. I knew she had plans for winning over the remainder, but she would always have enemies. Jo and I knew there were always a chance some troublesome fae could show up.

Morrigan welcomed us when we popped out on a sidewalk in Galway. She was dressed in brilliant white, with a crystal necklace of watermelon tourmaline, half a brilliant red-pink and the other half a bright emerald color. Disconcertingly, her eyes matched the necklace – one bright green, the other bright pink-red. Morrigan nodded at me in approval per my similar dress and eye-style. I could see Jo's smirk.

Then Morrigan welcomed Jo and bent down slightly to welcome Isabel. Morrigan's long black hair was a perfect contrast to the white jacket. I realized how stunning she was, in a different way than Jo, and realized they had dressed to impress each other.

Fine with me, I didn't mind spectating. Just as I was thinking that I noticed Jo give me a warning look. She could read my mind ever since she had gotten the Danu essence and become immortal, or close to it.

The four of us gathered closer and clasped hands, and Morrigan popped us to the realm. The diamond ceiling was always a treat and right now was showing a brilliant blue with a few white "clouds" floating over. The realm was not Christian but celebrated their holidays in a similar manner of colors and gift-giving, based on traditions of the season. Colors of the realm this year were predominately green, red, gold, silver, and white, while one section of town was only decorated in a dozen shades of blue to celebrate an ice princess. The fae realm tended to change color schemes each year, with green the only color always in use.

We walked and shopped in a several stores that Morrigan recommended. I trusted her when it came to Isabel's safety, plus I knew Jo was keeping watch on everything. The first shop was a mixture of jewelry, watches, and small appliances. Of course, this was the fae realm so none of the items was exactly what humans would expect.

Isabel zeroed in on a pair of earrings at the counter. Tiny golden things resembling a fae version of dragonflies. But these earrings, although they appeared gold, really were buzzing and began flying around. One landed on each of Isabel's ears and lightly held there.

"Mom, these are great, can I get them?"

"I don't know dear," Jo answered. "Morrigan, are these alive or mechanical? I'm not sure we would want to own something that was alive."

"Oh, they are alive and wear the gold shell for protection," Morrigan said. "But you don't own them; in fact, they adopt you. In this case, they were attracted to Isabel's nature and have chosen her. If she wants them, they will stay with her for a year, although she can bring them back anytime if she changes her mind. After a year they mate, lay two eggs in water, and then die. Once hatched, the two new auriculas move into the gold shells. They are free to adopt Isabel again or move on to another if they choose."

"What do they eat?" I asked.

"At night they stay in the room and feed on small insects, mostly things like mosquitos and spiders. Keeps your room very clean and no cobwebs."

"OK Isabel, you've heard about them," Jo said. "Do you still want them?"

"Yes please," Isabel answered. She wore them out of the shop and for the next year.

We hit another dozen stores and saw a few hundred interesting and amazing things you couldn't see anywhere else. One shop had a pot with frozen bright flames a foot tall. Other pots had shorter flames, and some appeared empty.

"These are phoenix fungi," Morrigan said. "They appear as a flame and get to full size in two weeks. Isabel, touch this mature one with the full flames." Isabel did and it made a laughing noise and fell to dust in the pot. Isabel looked uncertain for a second but then laughed as Morrigan said "It will grow back in two weeks and then fall again."

Another shop was full of various soaps, scents, lotions, and other sundries for the body. Isabel found a tube of what looked like lip gloss.

"Here Isabel, try this," Morrigan said. "Now think of a color or pattern." Isabel's lips turned bright purple for a moment, morphed into leopard spots, then became a tiny green lawn. She laughed while looking in the mirror. I tried it and my lips became a closed zipper. Both Jo and Morrigan nodded approval.

Ultimately, Isabel was so pleased with her earrings she did not ask for anything else. Jo got a lovely silk scarf that changed patterns and colors depending on the clothes worn with it. I ended up with a bicycle bell that made random farting noises, but when triggered would loudly yell funny insults in an Irish accent. I looked forward to riding with it on my bike in Vondel Park.

We went to the ice cream store we had visited previously. They had every imaginable holiday flavor, plus a new favorite for the kids called "ice princess," that turned your face blue and hair white for a few minutes. Isabel had to have it. I found a new favorite, a hot chocolate drink that turned to ice cream in my mouth. A very odd sensation at first but one I quickly learned to appreciate. Jo tried "chunky monkey" and got quite a surprise. An animated chocolate monkey sat on her chin and alternated throwing little balls of banana or peanut butter ice cream into her mouth, then jumped in afterward. It was quite amusing but a little too realistic for me.

A few hours of fun and we bid goodbye to Morrigan and the fae realm. We went to Amsterdam to my house on the canal. We planned to stay a few days to see the city with Isabel, check on things at the Woerden apartment, and possibly travel to a Christmas market. There were several good ones to choose from, but we liked the one in Bruges. It was small but had a distinctive setting. We would then travel to the UK to spend three days with Jo's family and the myriad of Isabel's cousins. Boxing day was going to be loud, confusing, and lots of fun for the kids.

Later that night I thought I heard something rustling on the roof. I reached out with my other sense and caught a hint of a presence, but no threat. I had not lived for 1700 years by ignoring things like this, however. Perhaps something had followed us back from the fae realm.

I got off the sofa to put on my shoes and jacket when Isabel came in the room. "Dad don't hurt it. It is not what it seems."

"OK, I'll just go check on it."

"I'll go get mom. Invite him in," she replied.

I should have known that she already knew what was happening. Just another odd evening in the land of the special paranormal pre-teen. I padded up steps to the third story and climbed out a window, on the other side of the house from our visitor that seemed to be on the rooftop terrace. I scrambled up the cold, slick slate tiles to the roof peak and peered over. There was something crouching on the rooftop deck just below me.

Despite my lack of a threat alarm and Isabel's words, I thought surprise was called for. Plus, I could be a ninja like Jo, assuming I didn't slide off the roof. I sprang over and dropped beside the figure, then grabbed what I thought was its arm. It squeaked and tried to jerk away, but I held firm. The arm was thin but muscular under thick hair. It kept trying to get free, but I was slightly stronger and held onto it. It straightened and was a lot taller than I had originally thought. Even in the dim light I glimpsed a ruin of a face set in a mass of hair with bright eyes. It sensed my revulsion and quit struggling, the tension leaving its body.

"You've caught the ugly thing then," he said. "Throw me off the roof and be done with it." The voice was so sad and dejected it took me aback.

"I apologize for my reaction. That was rude of me."

"You would apologize to me, a loathsome trespasser?" His eyes were large with surprise.

"I would and I do. I reacted poorly. But now tell me, why you are on my roof this evening?"

"I heard rumors the princess was visiting the city. I crept up here to see for myself."

"Princess? Ah, you must mean Isabel. She knew you were here and asked me to be nice to you."

"She did? The princess knows and thinks well of me?"

"I believe she does. Please come inside and meet her."

"Oh no, I can't! She will be frightened of me."

"Nonsense, she will be happy to see you. I insist, come inside as our guest."

The guest designation worked. It was common that supernatural creatures calmed and reacted well when given guest status. He stood even taller and straightened his rough clothing, which appeared to be a green burlap shirt and brown burlap pants. He seemed completely covered in coarse hair on all visible parts. I thought he resembled a rougher, smaller version of Kal's people, the American Bigfoot.

We entered the sliding door and went downstairs. I felt no ill will in him, only an excitement at meeting Isabel. By the time we got downstairs to the dining and kitchen area, Isabel and Jo had already set out a bar full of snacks and appetizers. Isabel had obviously briefed Jo on our visitor. Some time ago I had noticed that both Isa and Jo had uncanny abilities to evaluate threats, and when together they were even more powerful. I'd learned to trust their instincts completely.

Jo said hello with warmth, without cringing at his face like I had. He said hello back, then bowed slightly in front of Isabel without saying anything. She stepped forward and grabbed his hand and led him over to the food. "Please stay and eat with us," she said.

He seemed to tear up but nodded his head yes. We all sat at the bar and began chatting, occasionally asking our guest questions. The first hour we polished off most of the food and glasses of water and cider. I made some mulled wine which he seemed to like. It took some time, but he finally opened up and told his sad tale.

"My people came from the old forests of Europe. Few of us are left, as we are as diminished as the great trees in which we used to live. We now stay on the rooftops in the winters. It is not so bad. We can be warm near the chimneys and usually are safe if we stay quiet."

"There are lots of stories of those that land on the roof and use chimneys this time of year," Jo said.

"Yes, but all those tales were garbled over the years. It started centuries ago when the farmers sometimes did terrible things to survive the harsh winters. It was easier for humans to blame ugly creatures like us when children died or disappeared after the food ran out on isolated farms. Then we were confused with St. Nicholas, because of the myth where he landed on the roof and entered houses through the chimney. Here in Holland, we were even confused with Zwarte Piet and tricking or tormenting children. But for all that, it has always just been us, first in the trees and then on the rooftops."

"That is sad," Isabel said. "But you can come visit us whenever you want to."

"Thank you," he said, as he teared up again. And that was our first dinner, but not our last, with the Krampus.

Krampus said it was time for him to go so we said our goodbyes. He asked to borrow a glass and I agreed. We walked together back upstairs and out onto the rooftop patio.

"I cannot thank you enough for your hospitality," he said. "You have honored me tonight, and my people and me will guard your roof wherever you are on this continent."

"Thanks, Krampus. We will leave a plate of food and stein of mulled wine as a thanks, or your people can come in for a snack."

"A plate and mug outside would do nicely. And I have a gift for you before I go." He pulled out a small knife from a hidden pocket. I watched as he cut the inside of his forearm and then held the borrowed glass underneath to catch the blood. He handed the glass to me as he pulled out a rag and bound his arm.

"Um, I'm not sure where this is going, but we don't usually drink blood from guests."

He looked at me strangely then laughed. "Oh no, that is for your lab. You have heard of the myth of werewolves battling vampires, yes?"

"I have heard of that, mostly through books and movies."

"It is a myth because werewolves don't battle vampires. My people do, which is why we are so few. The vampires hate us because we are poison to them. Our presence torments them and our blood kills them quickly. My gift to you tonight for your hospitality is my blood, so that you may find its secret and have similar success against those creatures."

"Krampus, rarely has anyone ever offered me such a gift. My great thanks to you." He smiled, bowed, then sprouted wings from under the burlap shirt somehow, and dropped off the edge of the roof.

I hurried downstairs to put the blood in a vial to refrigerate it. In all my years I'd never been given blood as a holiday gift. But this was a great one, and one to be shared. Tomorrow morning I'd take it to Michael so he could get it to his lab. But first, just to mess with him, I'd tell him it was a holiday breakfast drink.

Epilogue

I have family that I love, wonderful friends, and trusted colleagues and companions. The world is still unsettled and filled with undesirable characters, all trying to create havoc for their own gain. But I have hope that everything will work out. I don't know that for sure, but I have a deep sense that although there will be dark times, we will survive and prosper. Hell, it took Danu more than 60 million years to get where she is, so I figure it may take us a while too.

Besides, I know of a powerful secret weapon that the world has not seen yet. A beautiful little girl with the potential to change the course and destiny of humanity, perhaps even this whole sector of the galaxy. Sounds like a good story in the making. But that is for another time. Right now I'm taking Jo and Isabel to the village green, here in beautiful Danu Valley, for a movie and ice cream with our friends.

About the Author

I've been doing this writing thing for a few decades now, but fiction is a new gig. I'm still learning, but it seems to involve having a lot of weird thoughts and the willingness to type them and inflict on others. If you made it this far, consider yourself infected with the Fisher of Time.

My name is Doug Smith. Officially I'm using Douglas P. Smith, Ph.D., because there are a multitude of Smith authors, including Doug Smiths, even in science fiction. Now living in Asheville and enjoying the mountains after several dozen other places. The most memorable being the Netherlands, and hope to return someday, at least part-time. I guess that is where this madness started, walking the midnight cobblestone streets of Woerden in a snowfall. The town square, or kerkplein, sits on the site of a Roman garrison. One of those ghosts seeped into my brain, and here we are. The ghost traveled with me around the world and the result is this series of books.

If you like any of this book, please consider leaving a rating, or better yet a review. If you have questions or run across an editing issue, email me at doug@douglaspaulsmith.com or dougsmith.author @gmail.com. I also have a website at douglaspaulsmith.com. Thanks for reading.